WATCHER

A RAVEN PARANORMAL ROMANCE

STEFFANIE HOLMES

BACCHANALIA HOUSE

Want free books, exclusive giveaways and exclusive sneak peeks at upcoming Steffanie Holmes paranormal romance books? Sign up for the mailing list to get the scoop.

❀ Created with Vellum

A TASTE OF WHAT'S TO COME

"Argh, stop it!" I yelped, as Cole reached up and rubbed the flour through my hairnet, smearing it all down my cheeks and over my shoulders. As I reached up to slap him away, he grabbed me under the arms and picked me up, pushing me back so I was sitting on the bench, legs open around him, our faces just inches apart.

All thoughts of struggling fled from my mind, along with the voice that was screaming at me that this was a bad idea. I became aware of just how close we were, my breasts were nearly touching his chest, his crotch was only an inch from mine. All I could see, all I could *feel*, was Cole, the warmth of his body, his eyes boring into mine ...

"Hey," he whispered, his voice hoarse. His lips dangerously close to mine. His breath tickled my skin.

"Hey," I whispered back. My heart hammered against my chest. The blood rushed in my ears. *Please, kiss me ...*

1

BELINDA

*T*he moment I saw Finn pull the tray of sweet-smelling Eccles cakes from the oven and pick up the bowl of pink icing, I knew both our lives were in serious danger.

Well, perhaps that was an exaggeration. Finn's life was definitely in danger, because if he touched the knife he'd just dipped in pink icing on to one of those pastries, I was going to kill him. But my existence was probably safe. I mean, I was smaller than Finn, so when I tried to stuff a sultana-filled Eccles cake down his throat, and hold his mouth and nose shut until he stopped struggling, there was a slim chance he might be able to overpower me and shove my head into the oven. But, he was also a gangly, unco-ordinated teenager, and I was a baker with muscles hardened from years of kneading dough, running on nothing but caramel syrup and righteous indignation. He didn't stand a chance.

The real danger to my own person was what would happen when the authorities came to investigate Finn's death and found me performing a celebratory dance around his prone corpse. And these days, first time murderers got off pretty lightly. My best friend was a lawyer. I was sure I could sweet-talk a judge into letting me off with just community service. In fact, if you asked my regular customers, they might say that choking Finn to death with an Eccles cake counted as a public service.

I sighed, tossing aside the joyous image of my assistant lying dead in a pool of pink icing, and bit back the urge to scream. I grabbed the knife from his hand and held it away from the tray. "No, Finn. As I *already* explained, the Chelsea buns need to be glazed *now,* while they're hot, but those Eccles cakes stay naked. They're filled with sugar and sultanas, that's sweet enough."

"OK, sure." Finn grinned. He promptly picked up the bowl of dripping sugar glaze and started spreading it over the Eccles cakes again.

I turned away from the kitchen disaster, trying to force down the tears that were now threatening to spill down my cheeks. This wasn't funny anymore. That was a whole tray of Eccles cakes ruined, unsaleable. And right now I needed every sale I could get.

You can't expect so much from a fifteen-year-old, I told myself, trying to calm down. *You have to cut him some slack. It's not his fault he's going to be the nail in the coffin of your business.*

Finn had been working as my shop assistant for the last three months, and for a fifteen-year-old boy, he definitely displayed a healthy dose of enthusiasm. What he didn't display was any ability to follow instructions, nor even the most basic aptitude in the kitchen. And since I owned *Bewitching Bites,* a busy bakery located on the high street of Crookshollow specialising in traditional British Cuisine (don't laugh, it's a thing), every incorrectly glazed sweet treat meant a disappointed customer.

I'd started *Bewitching Bites* three years ago, at the insistence of my then-fiancé, Ethan. It had been my lifelong dream to own a bakery, but I'd always been too afraid of failure to do anything about it. My beloved grandmother had died and given me a small inheritance, and Ethan had cornered me about the money. "This is your one shot to make it work, Belinda," he said, squeezing my hand. "It's time you did something for yourself. I'll help you every step of the way. I've run my shop for years. I know everything you need to know about retail. And, with your culinary talent, we'll make it work."

And so, buoyed up by his confidence in me, I'd leased a small space on the Crookshollow high street where an old Indian take-away had once been, spent two months scrubbing the curry smell out of the kitchen, and set about planning a menu of savoury and sweet treats to delight the populace of the village. Since Ethan had run his own successful auction house for several years, I'd gone to him with every business question I had. He put me on to his accountant Clive, his business advisor and even his sign writer.

Of course, what I hadn't realised at the time was that Ethan and his accountant Clive had been running a money-laundering scam, using the auction house as a front. Of course, all the signs were there: Ethan's caginess about some of his clients and private sales, Ethan's general lack of knowledge about old, valuable objects, Ethan's expensive car, designer clothes and gold watch, which he seemed to have no trouble paying for, and yet when it came to bills or dates with me, would always claim his money was tied up in "investments". Then there was Ethan's reluctance to share any of his documentation or phone conversations or even allow me to clean his office, and his overconfident demeanour whenever he was in the presence of the police ... But I'd ignored the signs. Who needed signs when we were in love and building a flourishing business empire?

Well, it turns out, the signs turned into a big raging billboard that read CRIMINAL SCUMBAG: STAY AWAY. If only I'd seen the billboard before Ethan had cleared out my bank account, ran up a large tax bill in my name, and skipped town with most of my worldly possessions.

At the time we rented a nice apartment a block away from the main street, and I'd just returned from a long shift at the bakery. I walked in the door, and went to put my keys on the table, but the table wasn't there. Nothing was there. Not the TV, not the sofa, not the pictures on the walls. Ethan had taken the food from the kitchen, and my clothes from the wardrobe. He'd even deprived Chairman Meow – my fat, cantankerous tortoiseshell cat – of his cat igloo.

He didn't leave a note.

I was still sitting in the middle of the barren living room, trying to make sense of what happened, when the police came knocking. Detective Sanders and Sergeant McCalister were perfectly lovely for officers who clearly suspected I'd tipped Ethan off that he was about to get busted. They'd closed down my shop for six weeks while they investigated my books, further compounding my financial woes. Eventually, they'd concluded I was just another of Ethan's victims – instead of his accomplice – but until they found Ethan, there was very little they could do. And even if they *did* find him, Detective Sanders warned me in his quiet, sad voice, I'd be unlikely to see any of my money or possessions again. Last I heard, they'd traced Ethan and Clive to a bank account in Liechtenstein. That was a small country, so you wouldn't think he'd be difficult to find, but apparently Liechtenstein's entire GDP relies on them being able to reliably hide both ill-gotten money and the people who obtained it.

At least I still had the shop, my beloved shop. But now I owed HMRC three years in unpaid taxes, plus fines. The debt had eaten away at my small monthly profit margin, and even though the bakery was thriving, I couldn't see any way out of my dark tunnel of debt. I'd already cut out all the unnecessary financial burdens, giving up the swanky apartment to live in the tiny hovel above the shop. I'd cut the three employees I'd hired to run the whole shop myself. I'd even stopped using the expensive stone-ground organic flour I loved because it cost an extra 30p per pound. That had bought me enough money to sustain myself, but it wasn't enough. I knew I had to do something to change the situation, but I couldn't see how. The whole thing just seemed so hopeless.

In seven more years you'll be free of the debt, I reminded myself, trying to stay positive. *Seven more years, and you'll be able to hire staff and get manicures again.*

"Hey, Belinda."

The familiar voice called from inside the shop. I looked up from the kitchen, relieved to see a friendly face regarding me with concern from across the counter. It was Elinor Baxter. She'd recently moved to Crookshollow from London, where she'd once been a solicitor at a prestigious London firm. Now, she was doing an apprenticeship as a tattoo artist with my other friend Bianca Sinclair over at *Resurrection Ink.* The two professions seemed at total odds with each other, but when you knew Elinor's story, they made perfect sense.

Elinor had a real sweet tooth, and she came into the bakery most mornings to grab something for breakfast and some sweet treats for her clients. We'd become good friends, and she'd introduced me to Bianca and their friend Alex. We had a great time together, although I saw them less and less now that the bakery was in such peril. After spending so many years with only Ethan for company, it was great to have girlfriends again.

"Hi Elinor." I poked my head out the kitchen door. "Come back here if you like. I've got some glazed Eccles cakes fresh from the oven if you want to try one."

"Glazed Eccles cakes?" Elinor swung around behind the counter and joined me at the long, stainless steel bench I used for finishing work. She grabbed one of Finn's iced cakes from the tray and stared at it with a pained expression. "If this is one of those culinary mashups designed to redefine English cuisine, I'm not sure I'm going for it."

"Me neither," I groaned, my chin sinking onto my hands.

"Are you okay? You look stressed."

"I'm not stressed." I moaned. "Do I look stressed?"

"People who aren't stressed don't usually hold their head in their hands as if it might at any moment roll from their shoulders."

I laughed uneasily. Even though we'd only known each other for a few months, Elinor had a knack for being able to tell when I wasn't being completely honest. I think it was her lawyer's instinct, instantly being able to deduce when someone was being truthful.

I hadn't told any of my friends about my current situation. They knew Ethan had left me and that I was struggling a bit financially, but they didn't know the full extent of the problem. They'd never seen my bare flat, and I was careful to save a bit of money for our occasional nights out so they wouldn't notice how dire things were. I couldn't explain why I kept it secret, I just ... every time I tried to say something, my whole body froze up. I felt ... embarrassed. Alex had a thriving art career and a rich, hot boyfriend, Elinor had found her passion as a tattoo artist and was dating a bona fide rock star, and Bianca ran a highly successful business and was always sleeping with someone hot and interesting. And what did I have? A mountain of debt and the knowledge that I couldn't pick a decent guy out of a lineup. Ethan had probably been in a lot of lineups.

So I did my best to keep up a sunny disposition. I knew that Elinor was suspicious about what was really going on, because she'd been asking a lot of questions about the shop and my life lately. But, when I thought about telling her, a huge knot tied up my chest. I wasn't ready for her to think me a failure. Not yet. Not until I really had no other choice.

"I'm fine." I sat up, trying to keep my smile bright. "No one's died. Nothing's burned down. I still have all my limbs." I pretended to check my legs. "See? Everything's intact."

"I see that Finn is working today," Elinor said. Finn looked up from the kitchen and grinned at her, hiking up the backs of his baggy pants in a way he probably assumed was masculine, but was in fact, rather idiotic. He did this every time she came into the shop. With her sleek brown hair, wide hazel eyes hidden behind dark-rimmed glasses, and her luscious curves, Elinor was like a walking hot librarian wet dream come to life. And the corner of her new back tattoo peeking out from the sleeve of her t-shirt gave her a badass streak that any teenage boy would find irresistible.

"Yes, he is," I said. "Are you sure you wouldn't like a platter of delicious glazed Eccles cakes to take back to the shop? People who are being poked with needles multiple times for fun need to keep their strength up. I'll even give them to you for half price."

Elinor stared into the box I held out. "They have *pink* icing ..."

"Yes. Er... We're trying a new experiment." I raised my eyebrows at her, gesturing to Finn with my pinkie finger. "It failed."

Elinor looked pained. It had been her idea for me to advertise at Crookshollow High School for a part-time staff member. After a month of trying to run the place completely on my own, it became clear to me that I simply couldn't do all the work there was to do, still manage to sleep for five hours a night, and not end up in a padded cell trying to eat my own elbow. The only problem was that, even at minimum wage, I couldn't afford to pay an assistant for more than a couple of days a week. Luckily, the government didn't consider teenagers in the same realm as actual people (and after hiring Finn, I came to understand why), so I could get a student in for a fraction of the price.

Finn was here as part of the school's "Work Experience" programme, for kids who were going into the trades or who planned to drive forklifts or sell sexual favours for a living. Instead of doing a class in mathematics, or aeronautical engineering, or advanced selfie photography, or whatever it was his peers who actually had two brain cells between their ears did, Finn came in three afternoons a week to make my life miserable.

Some of this pain must've come across on my face, because Elinor plonked down her wallet. "I'll take the lot," she said decisively, dropping the rest of her glazed Eccles cake into the rubbish. "My clients will be so busy figuring out why their Eccles cake is glazed, they won't even notice when I start stabbing them."

"That's the spirit!"

"But I'll also take a Cornish pastie and one of your gooey chocolate brownies. They're not glazed today, are they?"

"No, Finn hasn't quite got to those yet." As I rang up Elinor's purchase, the shop bell jingled. I looked up to see who had come in, and nearly dropped the EFTPOS machine.

The most handsome man I'd ever seen outside of a blockbuster action film strode through the door and up to the counter. Long dark hair that curled at the ends framed his strong face, and meltingly dark brown eyes – so dark they were practically black – scanned the room as if he were checking it for snipers. I saw the edges of a tattoo peeking out from the collar of his leather jacket. He wore dark jeans and huge, heavy boots that clanged as he walked. Under his arm, he carried a red motorcycle helmet, and I noticed a strange black ring encircling the index finger of his right hand.

I imagined that under those leathers was a toned, muscular body and more tattoos. Lots and lots of tattoos. I wondered what it would be like to run my hands over his muscled chest, feel the hardness of his pecs and abs, see the colours of his ink shifting before my eyes as he moved on top of me, making love with an intensity that left us both breathless ...

... *Ahem. Focus, Belinda.*

Clearly, I was more than ready for a sexual memory that didn't involve Ethan.

I gulped, straining to think of something intelligent to say. I'd always been attracted to bad boys, but I'd never had one, unless you counted Ethan: the skinny, petulant, thieving bastard. He didn't have a single tattoo, and he was too afraid of driving to even get his license. I had to drive him everywhere. So he didn't really count.

What was this *particular* bad boy doing in my bakery? He didn't seem the type to go in for my caramel whips.

The window for appropriate store-owner / customer interaction came and passed, and still my tongue was glued to the top of my mouth. Hot Biker Dude met my gaze, those smouldering eyes burning into mine. His whole face broke out into a startling, brilliant grin, the kind of smile that melted glaciers and left girls like me in puddles on the floor. I could feel my cheeks burning with heat. *Say something.*

"Wh-wh-what can I get you, sir?" I managed to stammer out. Across from me, Elinor giggled. I shot her a filthy look.

"What can you get me?" Hot Biker rubbed the stubble on his chin, his eyes darted over my face and across my body. "You can get me off with those pretty lips, if you like."

Did he just say ...? Behind me, Finn cracked up laughing. As his words registered, I felt my whole body blush. From the tips of my toes right up to the ends of my hair, my body coursed with heat. As much as his crass attitude annoyed me, I couldn't help but wish I had the guts to say, "Sure. Your place or mine?"

Hot Biker's line hung in the air between us, an open invitation to respond, to crush him with my unbelievable wit, to impress him with my ability to rise to his challenge. I swallowed. *Nothing.* My mind was a blank slate.

"Excuse me," Elinor cut in. "You shouldn't talk to her like that." *Great, now I look so weak I need to have my friend stick up for me.*

"Why not?" Hot Biker leaned over the counter and studied my face with those dark eyes. I don't know how it was possible, but my cheeks flared with even *more* heat. "She looks as if she's enjoying it."

"I—" I stammered, finally managing to croak out a sound. Unfortunately, I was too late. Elinor was in full no-bullshit mode.

"Well, for starters, Belinda is the *baker*. If you piss her off, she might put something unsavoury in your cupcakes."

"I'll take my chances." Hot Biker grinned at me; that wild, carefree grin that made my knees go weak. "Besides, your friend can talk for herself, can't you, gorgeous?"

"I ..." I cleared my throat. "Yes, I can, thank you. Do you want to order something?"

Good, that's good. Let's just get down to business. That should help you stop thinking about how hot he is. There's nothing sexy about pastries.

Unless he was feeding you a cupcake, pulling off small bites with his fingers and placing them on your tongue, licking his lips in anticipation as he imagined running his tongue over yours, smearing the icing around your—

Urgh. Who *was* this person thinking this stuff? My whole body pulsed with heat. I needed to get this guy out of here so I could go stick my head under the cold tap.

But Hot Biker wasn't in a rush. He leaned across the counter, his leather jacket creaking as he stooped to admire all the slices and sweets in the display

"You've got angel food cake," he grinned. "That's one of my favourites. Innocent on the outside, but full of naughtiness inside."

"Um ..."

"Is that like you, gorgeous?"

"I ... er ..." Scratch that, I think I needed a cold *shower*.

Elinor shot Hot Biker another filthy look. He rolled his eyes at her, then gave me a conspiratorial smile that made my heart hammer against my chest.

"Look at her!" Elinor jabbed a perfectly manicured finger in my direction, making my blush glow deeper. "You're making her really uncomfortable. Why don't you just place your order without being a fuckwit and then you can leave."

Hot Biker looked taken aback for a moment, but then he

nodded. He leaned across the counter, his brown eyes wide now, kinder.

"Listen," he said, his voice low. "I'm just teasing. The truth is, I came in to get something for brunch, but then I saw you behind the counter and that first line just came out. You looked so gorgeously flustered, I just wanted to see how long I could keep going. I wasn't trying to embarrass you."

"That's okay," I said, my face still burning.

"It's *hardly* okay." Elinor snapped. I shot her a frantic look, and she nodded, finally understanding that I was actually keen on the biker. She took a few steps back and hid her face in one of the newspapers I kept stacked by the door.

"Your friend is right." Hot Biker pulled out a fat leather wallet and started to flip through it. I noticed he was carrying a huge wad of cash. "I was acting like a dick. I'll tell you what, I'll take a box of the most expensive, most impressive treat you have. If you have to endure my sense of humour, than you should at least be fairly compensated for it."

"Really sir, that's okay—"

"Sir?" He gave me that killer grin again. "I like that. I don't usually get called Sir. You could definitely keep calling me that."

"So um ... anyway," I directed my gaze down at the display counter so he couldn't see the fresh glow on my cheeks. I pointed to a cake on the bottom shelf. "If you want the most impressive thing, that would definitely be the Heaven & Hell cake."

"That sounds like my kind of cake. Tell me about it."

"Well um, it's layers of Angel food cake and Devil's food cake, sandwiched with peanut butter mousse and covered with chocolate whisky ganache."

I'd made that cake last night to replace another that hadn't sold for three days – the full cakes didn't sell as well as individual slices, but I needed them on display to get the catering and birthday orders. I'd decorated it perfectly, with curls of dark chocolate and a sprinkling of gold dust. And I knew it was delicious, because I'd eaten a quarter of the other Heaven & Hell cake for dinner, since I couldn't afford groceries.

"Looks great." He wet his lower lip in a way that made my stomach flutter.

"I can cut you off a slice—" I reached for the cake knife.

"No, just box the whole thing up. I'll take it all."

"But ..." I spluttered. "That cake is 75 quid ..."

"That was more than I was planning on spending on our first date, but sure." He shrugged. "Wrap it up."

Barely able to hide my grin, I fitted together one of our larger cake boxes. I slid the cake out from the counter and had to turn around to fit it inside the box. As I did, I imagined Hot Biker staring at my arse, and my whole body coursed with nervous energy at the thought. When I turned around to give him the cake, I half expected to drop it. Thankfully, I maintained my composure.

He paid by credit card, and as I handed him the pen to sign his name, I found myself hoping he'd leave his number. If this were a movie, and I were the plucky, down-on-her-luck heroine, that's exactly what would happen.

Hot Biker grinned at me as he pushed the slip of paper back across the counter. This time, I grinned back. "That's a lot of cake," I managed to say. "I hope you have someone to share it with."

"Why? Are you free tonight?"

"Er ... um ..." My heart pounded. Was he asking me out? This guy was going to give me a serious heart condition.

He leaned forward, his nose just inches from mine. I could smell him, the scent of motor oil and leather and something else, something woody and earthy and familiar, but I couldn't quite place it. His eyes burned into mine.

"On second thought, you'd better not." He whispered, his voice suddenly cold. Disappointment surged through me. Where had that dark stare come from? Emotion flared in his eyes, and for a moment his face crumpled into an expression of impossible sadness. I blinked, but in an instant his smug, dangerous expression was back.

"You've been hurt badly." His husky voice reverberated in my skull. "You need something sweet, and I'm not just talking about cake. I am not sweet, not even close. You wouldn't want to get messed up with a guy like me."

He grabbed his cake off the counter, and stormed outside, the bakery door slamming shut behind him.

"Woah," Elinor slapped down her magazine. "Who the hell was *that?*"

"I don't know. He's never been in here before." I stared down at the slip where he had scrawled his unreadable signature. No name. No phone number.

Elinor marched over to the counter and waved her hand in front of my face. "Hello? Are you in there?"

"I'm sorry," I blinked. "I just ... I was hoping he'd ask me out."

"Belinda," Elinor looked me in the eyes, her voice stern. "Don't go getting all doe-eyed for Mr. Smooth-Talking-Biker. You are clearly not over Ethan, and that guy would *not* help. He's bad news. In fact, he even *told* you he was bad news. And the last thing you need is to date another criminal."

She had a very good point. Hot Biker was gorgeous, sure. He was probably an amazing shag. And, the way he looked at me made me feel fluttery all over, like I was actually attractive and desirable and not just a colossal fuck-up. I hadn't felt like that for a long time, not since I'd first started dating Ethan. But, what would I even talk to a guy like that about? I didn't have any tattoos. I'd never ridden a motorbike. All I had going for me was the fact that I always smelled like warm bread.

Elinor was right, that guy was bad news. Guys like him always were. I was glad he didn't ask me out or leave his number.

I *was* glad. Wasn't I?

2

COLE COLE COLE

W *oah.* I shook my head as I jammed the cake box into the pillion, and fitted my helmet over my head. She was *something else*. That wispy black hair, that creamy skin, those huge, sad eyes, the way she blushed adorably every time I said something dirty ... she was like an anime character, come to life. She wasn't just entirely fuckable, she was *intriguing*. And I hadn't been intrigued by a woman in such a long time. I glanced back through the window of the store, where the black-haired beauty was deep in conversation with her buxom friend. I had the overwhelming urge to run back in there, grab her over the counter, pull her face to mine, and kiss her.

You did the right thing, I reminded myself, as the ring on my finger brushed against the handlebar with a metallic CLINK. *No more women, no more distractions, especially not a distraction you might actually be interested in talking to. You have nothing to offer a woman like that until you are free.*

I gunned the engine, kicked up the stand, and pulled out into the street. I dared one last look back at the *Bewitching Bites* bakery, just in time to see the buxom friend leaving with a huge cake box under her arm. That meant my black-haired beauty was alone. Maybe I could head back and—

Someone honked. I stomped on the brake and slammed my foot down before the bike fell over, just as a car sped past and the driver pulled the finger at me. I'd drifted over the white line. *Fuck, that was close.*

Keep your eyes on the road. You wouldn't want to crash now, it might spoil your master's dinner.

As I pulled away again, I glanced wistfully in the direction of the *Tir Na Nog* pub, where I knew Mikael would be working the afternoon shift. It was too risky to go there now, when I knew Pax and Poe were nearby, also doing chores in the village for the master. If they saw me talking to Mikael, they might guess what we were doing, and I couldn't let anything jeopardise our plan. Not when we were so close.

I zipped through the quiet Crookshollow streets, keen to put some distance between me and the pub and the bakery. I needed to clear my head a bit. After a few minutes, the village died away, and I sped through winding country roads, the wind whipping my long hair against the collar of my jacket. The cold brushed my skin even through my leathers, momentarily blasting away my rage.

Out on my bike, I felt like myself. The wind tearing at my body, the road falling away beneath me, that powerful engine humming away between my legs ... it was the closest thing to flying in my human form. On the back of that bike, I felt almost free.

Almost.

All too soon, my ride came to an end. I saw the castle long before I reached the gate. It towered over the picturesque landscape like a tacky Hollywood mansion. Just like Victor Morchard, I thought snidely, grinning at the comparison.

I pressed the button on the handlebars, and the iron gates swung open. I entered the long gravel drive leading up to the main house, but turned off down a small track on the left, winding through rows of grapevines and maple trees. Our roost was located on the edge of the private forest that bordered the Morchard's estate, well hidden from the eyes of wandering National Trust visitors touring the castle.

I parked my bike in the lean-to at the base of the roost, then held my index finger up to the small electronic pad. It read the energy signature on my ring, and beeped twice to signal my return had been recorded. I checked the blinking symbols on the left of the screen. None of the others were back yet.

I didn't bother going up into the roost. There was only enough room up there for the four of us to sleep, and even then, only in our raven forms. Victor didn't like us to spend any more time than necessary in our human forms. I think he found us intimidating.

The ring on my finger grew warm. Morchard's call. He wanted to see me, immediately. Well, the bastard could wait. I took my time removing the cake from the pillion, and buffing out some imaginary scratches from the chrome on my bike. I slung my jacket over my shoulder, and ran my fingers through my hair, deliberately messing it up. The ring glowed hotter, and my whole hand stung with pain, but still I dawdled in the gardens, stopping to peel a grape from the vines and crush a small cluster of daisies under my boot.

I entered the castle through the servant's entrance, and left the Heaven and Hell cake on the counter in the kitchen. Two chefs clattered away over the stoves, yelling instructions at each other as they cooked for the meal the family were preparing to celebrate the arrival of their favourite son. Harry Morchard, the great hope of the family, was due home from university tomorrow. He was reading chemistry at Oxford, and he would no doubt take over his father's sadistic business.

At the thought of Harry, I almost swiped the cake box off the table and smashed it against the floor. He didn't deserve a cake like that. I didn't want that haughty git anywhere near *her* handiwork.

But I gritted my teeth, and walked through the kitchen, leaving the cake behind. Neither of the chefs bothered to look up. Who would acknowledge a slave?

My whole hand ached with pain now. Despite myself, I walked faster, cursing my weakness.

I knew where I would find my master. I stomped through the immaculate receiving rooms, the elaborately inlaid walls and painted frescos passing in a blur. At the back of the empty ballroom – the one decorated with wax figures dressed in pseudo-regency garb for the tourists – I pressed the hoof of a prancing horse inlaid on the wall panel, and the secret door swung open. I stepped inside.

Instantly, the heat in my hand faded, although it would take some time before the pain would also fade. I was in my master's abode.

Victor was hunched over his worktable, filling a syringe with some kind of clear liquid. In front of him on the table were three glass cages, each one housing a different bird. The first held a beautiful white dove, her eyes dilated, struggling to focus on me. The second, a common pigeon crying for release, and the third, a black raven, his hooked beak tapping nervously on the glass. Their cries wrenched my soul, but there was nothing I could do to save them. I nodded at Victor, keeping my composure, trying not to let him know how much I hated him.

"Ah, Cole. I'm glad you could join me. You certainly took your time getting here."

"I had to drop off the cake in the kitchens," I replied, keeping my voice even.

"Yes, good." He didn't look at me, his dark grey eyes concentrating on his work. His long, gaunt body hunched forward, his back curved like a geriatric as he filled two more syringes. I shifted my weight to my other foot, my whole body screaming to run away. This room, the sterile white walls, the ammonia smell that couldn't quite disguise the acrid stench of blood, the memories that flooded me every time I came in here ... it was as if Morchard knew how I felt, as if he was trying to keep the upper hand.

"You have some other task for me?" I asked, desperate to find out what he wanted so I could leave.

"You don't like me, Cole. And I've never been able to figure out why. I've done nothing but care for you as a part of my family. I've paid for your schooling, given you free reign over my grounds and the village, allowed you every privilege. I've provided a home for you and your brother. But you are ungrateful. You seek to defy me at every turn. I can sense your rebellious spirit under your skin every time I speak to you."

"You're my master. I obey your commands." My words came out as a rasp. My throat was closing up. The smell ... I couldn't take it much longer.

"I don't only demand obedience from my Bran. I demand devotion. Your mother understood that."

"Don't you speak of her," I growled, my hands balled into fists. The ring on my finger flared with heat.

"I'll not tolerate this insubordination any longer." As he talked, Victor lifted the lids to each of the cages, and injected each bird with one of the syringes. The dove fluttered her wings, and toppled on to her side, her eyes lolling sadly. The pigeon grew stiff, and flopped over with a THUD. And the raven folded its wings and sat down, its beak drooping against the glass. I was so focused on those poor birds that it took several moments for me to even register what Victor was saying.

"—and therefore, I have made the decision that you are to no longer stay here as a Bran of mine. I have sold you to another master. He has paid a fair price for you, enough that I've been able to wipe some of the debt my little laboratory has incurred.

He will come for you on Sunday, and the bond will pass from me to him at midday. This way, you won't be my problem any longer."

He *sold* me? He sold me like a piece of fucking property. Like I was a Chesterfield sofa or an ornamental urn.

Rage consumed me. I saw red. I wanted to scream at him, pulverise his thin face into pulp, fill one of those syringes and jab it directly into his eye, tip his stupid laboratory table on top of his head and stomp on it until he stopped screaming. But the ring on my finger surged with energy, sending slivers of pain up through the veins in my arm. My body went rigid. I couldn't fight it. I couldn't disobey him.

And so I'd stood there, silent as stone, as Victor informed me of my fate. And I hated myself for my weakness, for my inability to stand up to him, to fight through the pain. But at that moment, I hated Victor more.

"Who?" I managed to choke out. "Who will be my master?"

"I have sold you to Sir Thomas Gillespie," Victor looked up at me then, his cold hard eyes dancing with glee. "I think you will find him a much stricter, much more cruel master than I have ever been."

The very mention of that name filled me with a sudden, cold fear. Sir Thomas Gillespie wasn't just one of the most powerful men in all of England, the last in an ancient noble family. He was also one of the few remaining vampires in the country, notorious for his cruelty and indifference. He was the man who killed my father. I would no longer be ruled by a man of flesh and blood, but an immortal being of infinite cruelty.

"But you ... how could ... you hate Sir Thomas."

"I wanted to be rid of you, and he offered a fair price. My personal feelings for the man did not enter into it. You will perform your usual duties and watches until the end of the week, but you are forbidden to leave the castle grounds until Gillespie arrives to collect you, unless I give you permission. I won't have you trying anything desperate. Is that understood?"

Despite every muscle and sinew in my body struggling to prevent it, I nodded slowly, the words rushing from my mouth before I could stop them. "Yes, master."

"In the meantime, I want you to finish your watch for today and then head down to Oxford to escort my son home. I'd like for someone to watch him, make sure he doesn't get himself into any trouble. And don't think this is your chance to escape, for Harry is expecting you. He will hold you to your bond."

"Yes, master." Harry had learned cruelty from his father. He would make certain I knew my place.

"You may leave," Victor turned away from me. "Shut the door on the way out."

And just like that, I had been thrown from the only home I had ever known. I turned on my heel and stroke away, slamming the door shut with such force the entire wall shuddered in protest. A piece of the horse's mane broke off and clattered on the marble floor. What did it matter? What could Victor do to me now?

I raced through the castle, barely registering anything around me. My whole body surged with anger - my mind replaying the whole conversation over and over. How *dare* he?

By the time I got back to the roost, I was a ball of rage. The black panel beeped angrily at me, letting me know the others were on their way home, and that I was past due to start my journey down to Oxford to meet Harry. I balled my hand into a fist and punched the panel with all the force I could muster.

I yanked my hand back, wincing at the pain in my knuckles. A long, jagged crack appeared across the screen, trailing out to the edges in an impressive spider-web pattern. The panel beeped angrily, but the lights continued to glow.

My ring hummed against my skin, reminding me again that I should be on watch. Fine, if Morchard wanted me to *watch*, then that's just what I'd do.

I leapt on the bike again, jammed the helmet on my head, and steered the machine out of the grounds. I sped toward the edge of the county, toward the line of trees on the horizon. *The forest*. The one part of Morchard's estate that he could not entirely control, the only place in my tiny world that had some semblance of wildness.

I found my usual hiding spot out on the edge of Crook-shollow forest – a small, overgrown parking lot marking the start of one of the less-frequented hiking tracks. I parked up and turned off my bike, then wheeled it into the bushes and hid it underneath the shrubs. Glancing around to see if anyone was watching, I pulled off my clothes, and stashed them in the pillion. My hands shook. Was it with anger, or with fear, I couldn't tell.

I closed my eyes, and I forced myself to change.

It is said that a process of changing forms is a highly individual experience. No two shapeshifters will have the same sensations nor change in exactly the same way. My mother used to describe hers as a sensation of sinking into the ground, collapsing in upon herself like a toppling house of cards. For me, it was as if I were some living statue made of clay, unable to move or cry out as my maker rearranged my pieces and cut away at my limbs. The sounds disturbed me more than anything – the scrape and crunch of my bones recasting themselves, the hiss as my pores opened up to allow my feathers to grow through, the crinkle of my skin folding away to be rolled out again later. Ever since I was a child those sounds haunted my dreams.

Even in my raven form, I was still a prisoner. This body – built for stealth, for hunting – kept me a slave.

I opened my eyes again, and the world became new and strange once more. I saw more than just colour and light, the energy of the world bounced back at me, a wild cacophony of new sounds and sensations resonated within my skull.

I unfurled my wings and took off, heading along the path of my usual afternoon round patrolling the western edge of the Morchard estate, heading back in the direction of the city. As I flew, I thought of all the awful things Victor had done to me, all the crimes he'd forced me to commit in his name, and what he had done to my mother when she had most needed his help. I thought of the carefully laid plan Mikael and I had been working on for months, all the pieces nearly in place to ensure both our escapes from this life of servitude. I came to the spot where I was supposed to turn around and head south along the other boundary.

Instead, I just kept on flying.

At first I felt nothing but a euphoria. I had done it. I'd actually left. I'd gone rogue. After all these years of thinking and planning for it, it was as easy as flying in a straight line. I glided over the rolling countryside with a strange sense of power. My beak hurt from the un-ravenlike smile that pulled at it. I was a bird in the sky. What could Victor Morchard do to me up here? I was free.

I managed two miles off my usual flight plan before the pain kicked in. The ring tightened around my wing, making flying difficult, slowing my escape. As I flew further from the castle, waves of agony assailed my body, and within minutes I was panting, my feathers slick with sweat. I barely had the energy to move my wings.

I have to reach Mikael. He's my only hope.

Mikael would still be at the pub. I was four miles from Crookshollow village, and I wasn't sure I'd make it, but I had to try. My throat constricted, and I wheezed as I struggled for air. I dipped, my right wing collapsing under the tightening ring. I hurtled down, the road rising up toward me.

No!

I squeezed my eyes shut, and *pushed* with my mind, forcing my wings to respond to *my* commands, not the ring's. Slowly, too slowly, I broke through the pain, forcing my own muscles to obey me, moving my wings apart, spreading them wide, feeling the wind ripple through my feathers.

I opened my eyes just in time to see the individual stones in the asphalt hurtle into focus. I jerked my neck back, and rolled over, flinging myself toward the heavens once more.

That was close.

I sucked in my air, opening my wings as wide as I could and straightening my neck and back, making myself as streamlined as possible. Ahead of me, I could see the houses on the outskirts of the village, and the gleaming glass facade of the Halt Institute on the northern end of the high street. The faster I could get to Mikael, the less chance—

I *sensed,* rather than heard, the other bird behind me. I didn't have to turn my head to know who it was.

Where do you think you're going, Cole? Pax hissed in caw-tongue, the language of Bran. His words bit the air like teeth.

This is a very stupid thing you're doing, added Poe. Out of the edge of my eye I saw his sleek figure slide through the air beside me, moving closer, blocking my escape.

I couldn't believe they'd found me this quickly. Byron must've reported me missing when I didn't cross his path on his watch as I headed to Oxford. Probably he'd seen the smashed screen back at the roost, too. Byron was such a stickler for the rules. He couldn't possibly know that I'd been sold to the Gillespies already, but he probably thought I was having it off with some girl – a fair assumption considering my past behaviour. My thoughts drifted briefly back to the black-haired beauty in the bakery. I wasn't going to be getting off with her any time soon.

Just this once, I'd wished Byron would have left me alone. I darted my head from side to side, searching for him, but I couldn't see him nearby.

I'd known, of course, that Morchard would send the other Bran after me. It was one of the factors Mikael and I were trying to mitigate in our escape plan. Of course, I'd gone and shot the escape plan to shit, and now Pax and Poe flanked me, forcing me to fly lower and lower across the village.

Rows of brown-roofed terraces zoomed below me, growing

closer and closer as Pax and Poe pushed me down, down … I tried to turn against the wind, hoping to give them the slip, but the ring tightened around my skin, collapsing my wing and sending me into an uncontrolled spin.

I struggled to regain my balance. Out of the corner of my eye, I saw Pax dive for me, his talons pointing directly at my throat. I spun away, and his sharp talons snagged my leg. I cried out as he tore through my flesh.

My leg flared with pain. I heard something snap in my wing, and the whole side of my body went limp. The air around me changed, and suddenly I was no longer buoyed up by the hot currents.

I was falling.

Houses zoomed past me at odd angles, colours spun around me like some terrifying funhouse ride, but I knew it wasn't the world spinning out of control. I was the one flailing through the air.

Then my body slammed against something hard, and everything went black.

3

BELINDA

*U*sually, I kept the bakery open until 5:30, or whenever I sold out. But on Tuesdays – my slowest day – I shut the shop at 4PM. This gave me an hour in the village before the other shops close to get to the post office, do the grocery shopping, and make my deliveries.

The local authorities mandate that we're not supposed to sell anything that's freshly baked after a day, and no matter how carefully I planned, I usually had leftover food. Most of the other store owners in town dumped it in the rubbish, but I hated the wastefulness. So on Tuesdays I took a box of goodies over to the Crookshollow Rest Home, the Women's Refuge, or the homeless shelter. It was nice to spend an hour a week brightening someone else's day, it made for a pleasant break from staring down my own private tunnel of despair.

This week had been relatively busy, so all I had left were a couple of baguettes and three custard slices. Not enough to feed a horde of bored seniors or several mothers with excitable children. So I decided to go to the park. I knew some other creatures that would appreciate some free food.

Two blocks back from the Crookshollow high street was Fauntelroy Park, a large green space dotted with bright flower beds, towering oaks, a Tudor garden, some questionable sculpture installations, a beautiful Victorian gazebo, and a large pond filled with ducks. The land had been donated to the village during the 18th century by the Fauntelroy family – my friend Alex's ancestors – who'd owned a significant tract of land in the area. Now, the park was owned by the council, who kept it in excellent condition, installed cycle lanes and picnic tables, and posted large signs warning people not to fall in the pond. The park hosted a series of events throughout the year, including sculpture trails, Easter egg hunts, and a summer Shakespeare festival.

Since I spent most of my time holed up in the shop or my flat, I didn't get out much. Crookshollow village was surrounded on two sides by dense woods, and the rest of the landscape was picturesque rural views. It was the perfect village to begin a ramble, but I couldn't ramble while there were loaves to bake and Eccles cakes to ice.

But, I could get to Fauntelroy Park. Walking through the park never ceased to help me clear my head. Here, I felt calmer, as though all the problems eating me up inside were really quite manageable after all. There was something so peaceful about sitting beside the water, listening to the gentle ripples lap against the concrete edging. The air smelled fresh and sweet with the scent of the flowers. Birds sang in the trees, and the ducks and pigeons hopped excitedly all around. The Council liked to encourage other birds to frequent the park, and sometimes I even saw majestic ravens preening themselves beside the water.

It wasn't yet five o'clock, so most people were still at work, and the park was practically deserted. I found a seat on a bench not far from one of the most impressive oaks. The bench was only a few feet from the edge of the pond. *Perfect.* I ripped the first stick of bread into tiny chunks and threw it out at the ducks. They all leapt and squabbled for the scraps. One tiny bird kept grabbing the largest chunks he could find, only to have his elder siblings rip them from his mouth. Finally, he got so sick of it he hopped up on the bench beside me and started pecking at the other loaf. I laughed at his antics.

When was the last time you laughed? I asked myself, and a wave of sadness hit me. There hadn't been much to laugh about lately. Ethan had taken my sense of humour when he took my bed linen and all of my Monty Python coffee mugs.

My body sagged with exhaustion. I was only 23. I should be backpacking through Cambodia, or following a death metal band around Germany, or getting my pilot's license, or something equally frivolous and reckless. I thought again of my girlfriends, who were all pursuing their dreams with their dream men and having loads of fun. I had been working my ass off on my bakery dream of the last three years, and all I'd got for my efforts was a nightmare.

But what could I do? I still owed £15,000 on the credit card from Ethan's spending, and at least double that to the HMRC. I couldn't afford to hire anyone else. If I could somehow find the time to take on more catering jobs, I could replace some of the furniture Ethan stole. The shop was doing well, and as soon as I was out of debt, I could afford to ease up a little. But until then, I was trapped, and this tight, frightened feeling in my chest wasn't going to go away.

I wished I didn't feel so tired all the time, so stressed. Even when I collapsed into bed at night after twelve hours of non-stop work, I felt panicked, as though there were something more I should have done. I was too young to be tied to a job for 75 hours a week. But tied I was, thanks to my own stupid decisions.

My chest heaved, and I sucked in a couple of deep breaths, feeling a lump rise in my throat. I was dangerously close to bursting into tears. *Crying is pointless, Belinda. You've cried enough over Ethan already. It won't get the bills paid and the debt wiped. All that will do that, is hard work.*

I buried my face in my hands, dragging my feet up to my knees as I desperately tried to get my emotions under control. As I did this, I knocked the second baguette off the bench. I peeked through my fingers, watching as it rolled across the grass, gaining momentum as it headed toward the lake. All my duck friends waddled after it, diving for the water as the roll fell in with a *PLOP!* The ducks swarmed around it, my presence instantly forgotten as they tore at the loaf.

So much for my company.

I pulled out the other paper bag, and took out a custard slice. I was getting sick of my own baking, and the toll of subsisting primarily on pastry was starting to show around my stomach. But today I was having a hard time coping, and the interaction with the biker in the shop this morning had left me feeling strange and sad. His handsome face flashed across my vision, that cheeky smile, those smouldering eyes that betrayed a hint of sadness and pain beyond their mischievous sparkle. How would it feel to be desired by a guy like that? What would it be like to kiss those lips, feel that stubble against my skin, the tendrils of his hair falling over my face?

And why did his attitude change so suddenly? Why was he flirty one moment, and intense and sad the next?

I shouldn't even be thinking about him. He didn't want me. Of course he didn't. He'd made that perfectly clear. My cheeks burned at the memory of his remarks. He was probably still laughing about it as he drank Tennessee whiskey with his mates down at the pub. He could have any girl he wanted. Flirting was a game to him. And that wasn't a game I wanted to play.

But that sadness in his eyes, the pain raw on his face ... it had flickered there for a moment, but I had seen it. He knew my pain, because he'd been hurt by someone, too.

What had he said? "You've been hurt badly." Was it that obvious? Was Ethan's betrayal written all over my face, the way the biker's pain flickered over his?

I am not sweet, not even close. Maybe I didn't need someone sweet. Maybe what I needed was someone to fuck and forget, someone who could rid my head of all the painful memories of Ethan. Hot Biker could have done the trick, but he didn't want someone like me, someone "sweet." He probably wanted a succubus in leather.

The custard slice smelled so good. *What the hell. It's not as if a little sugar can make things worse.*

I took a big bite.

The creamy custard filled my mouth, exploding from the edges of the pastry and coating my hands. I'd forgotten how messy these things were. And how delicious. My custard was the proper homemade stuff, flavoured with real vanilla and a hint of lemon. It didn't come from a Sainsbury's packet mix, like other bakeries.

Croak, Croak!

Below me, I heard a strange squawk. At first I thought it must have been the ducks coming back to beg for a custardy dessert, but I could still hear them flapping about in the water as they tore apart the last of the baguette. Plus, this sounded nothing like a duck. It was more of a deep, throaty croak.

Croak! Croak! Crooooooack!

I heard it again, louder this time, more urgent. It sounded distressed. At first, I couldn't see where the noise came from, but then I noticed a large black lump hiding between the twisted roots of the oak tree.

I set down my dinner and went over to investigate. As I leaned over the lump, its shape became clear. It was a raven. I'd never seen one of the huge black birds so close before, and it was even more beautiful than I imagined. It was huge, nearly the entire length of my arm, and covered in smooth feathers that appeared to be made of black silk. A frill of shaggy feathers around its throat and above its beak gave the bird a distinguished, regal air. There was a black ring around the top of its wing, almost like some kind of tag. Its long, curved black beak turned and regarded me with a wide, watchful eye, then let out a tiny squeak, as if begging me to take pity on it.

"What's wrong with you, beautiful?" I asked. The raven tried to lift its wing, but could only move it a tiny bit. It hung its head, squawking again as if to assure itself that I was a friend. It was then I noticed the beautiful jet-black feathers around the wing were matted with blood.

"You poor thing," I cooed, as if the bird could understand me! Though my voice seemed to calm it, for it hung its head again, and with a squawk of effort, lifted the edge of its wing to reveal its leg. I saw a nasty wound near the top of the thigh, a long gash that was oozing blood. Many feathers had fallen out, and those that hadn't were snapped and coated with blood. It had clearly been attacked by something – a dog, perhaps? Sometimes people left their dogs off the leash in the park, even though the council signs prohibited it.

The bird blinked as its eyes followed my gaze, and it gave a sad *caw*. My heart broke to see such a beautiful creature in pain like that. *I can't believe some bastard let his dog do this and then just walked away and left the raven to die.* Well, I wouldn't leave the bird alone. I would get to do my good deed for the day, after all.

I glanced around me, but there was no one else in the park. Thinking quickly, I rushed back to the bench and grabbed the empty bread box. It would be a tight fit, but I should be able to get him (I was already thinking of the raven as a him, even though I knew nothing about raven anatomy) inside.

"Here you go, big guy." The raven's eyes followed me as I set the box down beside him. He didn't try to move as I pushed my fists into the ends of my jumper, shoved my hands underneath his body, lifted him gingerly from the dirt and placed him in the box. His feathers felt soft and silky through my jumper. He looked up at me with pain-filled eyes, and let out a little squawk of thanks.

"C'mon, boy. Let's get you out of here." I ran back to the seat, picked up my purse and threw the rest of the custard square to the ducks, then hiked back across the grass with my purse under one arm, and a squawking raven under the other.

I wasn't exactly sure what I was going to do with the raven, but I figured I'd get him back to my place first, and then figure out my next step. I should call the vet. *Yes, that's a good idea. Vets know about all sorts of animals, including parrots and chickens. A raven should be similar to a chicken, right?*

People gave me strange looks as I crossed the road and weaved through the streets with a large, croaking raven in a bread box. While I waited for the traffic light on Oxford West Street to turn red so I could cross, I fumbled one-handed in my purse for my cellphone, and dialled the local vet.

He picked up on the second ring. I took a deep breath, not certain how I was going to explain. "Hi Barry, it's Belinda Wu."

"Oh, Belinda, hello! I haven't seen you or Chairman Meow at the clinic for ages. I was meaning to tell you, those cat cupcakes you made for the RSPCA luncheon went down a treat. We're sponsoring a dog show in a few weeks and I'd love to chat to you about—"

"Yes, yes, thank you. I can definitely work something out if you get Carol to call me with the details. Listen Barry, I've got a bit of an emergency, and it's not the Chairman this time. I'm actually holding a raven."

"A ... raven?"

"Yeah, I'm on Oxford West, and I've got a raven in a box." My little black friend was becoming quite distressed with all the cars zooming past. His head whipped back and forth, and he started squawking loudly. A mother pushing a wailing baby in a pram glanced up at me with an odd look on her face. I gave her a shrug, as if we shared some kind of similar affliction, her with her baby and me with my corvid. The light turned red and I started walking slowly across the road, the phone pressed awkwardly between my ear and shoulder while I used both hands to steady the box. "I found him in Fauntelroy Park. Or she. I guess I don't really know much about raven genders. His leg is quite badly damaged. Can I bring him in?"

"Sure." Barry paused. "It's after hours, so—"

My heart fell. I could barely afford a vet visit, let alone an after-hours visit. "Um, right. Well, could you maybe help me out just this once? This isn't exactly my pet raven, you see—"

"Sorry, kid. I'm at home now, and Janice is pretty strict with the books these days, after everything that happened." Barry used to be a client of AE Accountancy, the firm owned by Ethan's friend Clive. So Barry had his own financial problems. "But I'll tell you what, if you keep that bird alive until morning, I'll come in 20 minutes early and see you first thing, and I won't charge you for the full visit. How would that work?"

"That would be great, except I don't know anything about nursing ravens."

"Just clean up the wound and make the bird comfortable. And keep him away from Chairman Meow. Do you have any antiseptic—"

A car honked loudly. I jumped. The raven squawked in terror, and managed to free its second wing from the edge of the box. With a flap, it toppled over the side and landed on the road.

"That's great, thanks Barry!" I yelped, and hung up. Heart pounding, I raced across the road after the bird as it had decided to make a run for freedom. I dived for the raven, but even with only one functioning wing it was fast. Its silky feathers slipped through my fingers, and it hobbled back toward the park, heedless to the traffic trying to come around the corner.

Please don't get run over, I prayed to whatever god was listening as I dashed back through the moving traffic. *I think Odin has something to do with ravens. Odin, please help us both get out of this alive.*

Now all the cars behind me were honking. The raven hopped toward the curb, squawking at the top of its lungs. A cyclist raced around the corner, and the bird barely managed to jump out of the way in time.

"Squawk!" The raven cried defiantly, raising a wing in the air and shaking it, almost as if it were expressing its indignation.

"What the fuck are you doing?" A driver called out as I stepped in front of him. Ignoring the honks and insults that were now pouring out of rolled-down windows, I lunged for the bird. He hopped out of the way at the last moment, limping directly into the path of another car.

"Just let me get my raven!" I cried to the driver, who slammed on the brakes just as I lunged for the bird again. This time, he flapped his wings and managed to hop a couple of feet in the air, hitting the car's radiator before coming crashing down again. As he tumbled across the curb, I managed to grab him, push his wings down, and shove him back in the box.

"Why would you do that, you idiot!" I growled, as I held the box tightly. The raven cooed in reply. Traffic poured through the intersection, drivers holding their middle fingers out the car windows as they hurtled past. My pounding heart slowed again. I was safe. The raven had lost a few more feathers, but was otherwise safe, too. Everything was okay.

I managed to get back to the shop without any other escape attempts. I unlocked the shop, and went straight up the steps at the back of the kitchen to my apartment. Chairman Meow greeted me at the door in his usual way, by wrapping his fat, fluffy body around my ankles and rubbing his face merrily against my legs. He stopped mid-rub as he noticed the box in my hands. His eyes grew as big as saucers. He stood on his hind legs and tapped the side of the box.

"CROAK!" The raven snapped back, flapping its working

wing madly. The Chairman darted away and hid behind the kitchen cabinet, his little nose twitching as he smelled the strange visitor I'd brought home. The raven flung itself madly in circles as it tried to hop out of the box again. Chairman Meow flattened his ears against the back of his head, and crouched low on the floor. This wasn't going to end well.

"Sorry boy, he's not for you." I set the box on the table, picked up the Chairman by the scruff of his neck, and locked him in the bathroom. He raked his claws against the door, loudly protesting my cruel treatment. How dare I deprive him of the most interesting thing to happen all week? He didn't want to kill the raven. He just wanted to be *friends*.

Which was probably true. Despite his name, Chairman Meow was a bit of a pacifist. He liked to chase butterflies around the alleyway out the back of the shop and watch the birds from the window, but he didn't have much interest in killing anything. Which was somewhat annoying, since I'd bought him from Barry originally because I thought he'd help keep down the mice population in the bakery. Instead, he liked to watch with saucer eyes from the top of the stairs while the mice made little white flour-trails across the kitchen below.

But the raven didn't know that, and it was going crazy, flapping its wings and trying to leap out of the box. Blood splattered from the wound in its leg, and I could see a pool of blood in the box underneath it. I needed to clean the wound before I did anything else.

I dug out the first aid kit from the cupboard and set it down on the counter. With one hand, I held the raven down as gently as possible, while I cleaned off the dried blood caked around the wound in the raven's leg. I noticed that black ring again. One of the local conservation groups must've been tagging the birds. I wondered if they'd come looking for him.

It was strange, but as soon as the raven saw me coming

towards it with the swab, it relaxed. It was almost as if the bird knew I was trying to help it.

Sadly, I wasn't sure how much I could do. Even after cleaning it, the wound looked pretty bad, and when I touched the skin around the cut, it felt hot. *Maybe I should take him to the vet after all?*

But then I remembered my overdraft, and the fact that the cupboard was nearly empty and the only furniture in the room was an electric frying pan and a couch I'd found on the side of the road. I had 100 quid left to last me the rest of the month. Even the vet visit was going to be a stretch, never mind an after-hours fee.

"I'm sorry, little guy ... or girl." I told the bird. "It's just your luck to be rescued by a hard-luck baker. But luckily, at least I have plenty of bread."

The raven croaked a reply. I almost imagined it saying, "That's okay. Now, tell me about this bread?"

I wrapped the raven's leg with some gauze, and left it hopping around on the table while I went downstairs to my storage area. I found a larger cardboard box, poked some holes in the top to serve as air vents, and lined it with paper. Then, I filled a saucer with water, and another with torn up bits of brioche, a few chopped nuts, a dollop of peanut butter, and half an apple. I found an old dishcloth under the sink, and bundled that up in the corner, making a kind of nest.

"Here you go," I set the box on the ground at the end of the couch and lowered the bird down into it. "I'm sorry it's not the Ritz, but it's got to be better than that tree in the park."

The raven nodded his head in agreement. He hopped over to the water dish and took a drink. I knew that was a good sign. Then, to my astonishment, the bird pecked at the peanut butter, smearing a streak down the side of his beak. He looked up at me, his beady eyes focused on mine, and I swear he gave me a kind of grin.

"So you like peanut butter, huh?" I leaned over and added another dollop to his bowl, then I spread peanut butter on the other half of the apple. That wasn't for the raven, but for myself. I sat down beside the box and chewed on the apple as I watched the bird explore his new surroundings. "So do I. I already like you better than my last boyfriend. He was allergic to nuts."

The raven regarded me with those piercing brown eyes. It nodded its head slowly. If I didn't know better, I'd think it was agreeing with me.

~

Now that the raven was safely in a proper box, I could let Chairman Meow out of the bathroom. He'd clawed a lovely long gash out of the moulding in his desperation to reach me, but as soon as I opened the door he jumped on top of the shower and started washing his paws, as if he couldn't care less what was going on outside. *Cats.* There was no sense in trying to understand them.

I set the raven's box on the stairs and kept an eye on him while I made batches of cookies, cupcakes and some chocolate eclairs for the following day. He let me feed him pieces of bread from my hand, and by the time I had finished he looked much healthier.

I glanced at my watch. 10:07PM. It was later than I liked to go to bed, but all the excitement with the raven had put me behind schedule. I still had food to prepare for tomorrow, but my eyes were already drooping, so I decided to just go to sleep.

I carried the raven back upstairs and set the box down beside the kitchen bench. I refreshed his water, and gave him another small lump of peanut butter. He seemed to have perked up a bit, and was even attempting to stand on his bad leg, albeit unsuccessfully. "You'll be okay out here for the night," I told him. "I'm going to shut Chairman Meow in the bedroom with me, so he won't disturb you. And in the morning, I'll take you to Barry and he should be able to fix you up good and proper."

The raven squawked in reply, nodded its head, and settled into the dishcloth. He stared up at me with those wide eyes, and I could almost imagine him telling me, "Goodnight."

Despite all my problems, for the first night in ages, I went to bed with a smile on my face.

4

COLE

*W*ell, this is an interesting development.
I paced around my large, dark box, my eyes having no trouble penetrating the gloom. I lifted my wing to examine my leg, and slid my beak over the feathers to clean a bit of dried blood off. She'd done a really great job cleaning it off. The wound no longer felt hot, now it just throbbed with a dull ache, which wasn't nearly as bad as the pain caused by the glowing ring, but even that I could ignore for now.

I was alive. It was a miracle. *If things keep going my way, and that cat doesn't eat me, I may just get out of here with my life.*

I couldn't believe I'd managed to escape from Pax and Poe. And now to end up here, warm and dry, and safe, with the woman I'd been fantasizing about ever since I laid eyes on her ... it was almost perfect.

The ache in my bones intensified. The ring around my wing seemed to shrink, constricting around me, reminding me that nothing could be perfect, not while I was a slave.

I hadn't planned to go rogue. Nothing was prepared. I didn't even know if Mikael would be able to find the witch ... and until he did, I had no way to break the spell that bound me to

Morchard. Or would bind me to Gillespie come Sunday. This pain was just going to keep getting worse, until eventually it consumed me completely.

But I just ... snapped. And now it was too late. I couldn't go back. I *wouldn't*. I would find a way to be free, or die trying.

I winced as my leg twinged. Pax really had cut me up bad. He was a good friend to have when he was on your side, but he was loyal to his master, which meant he was not someone I wanted to see again any time soon.

After Pax sliced my leg, I'd landed hard on the ground. I'd been stunned for a few minutes, unable to move or even open my eyes. I thought for certain they would have found me and finished me off, but by some miracle I'd fallen straight through the thick foliage of an oak tree, and now that same tree hid me from view. As soon as I could move again, I dragged myself further under the tree root just as Pax, Poe and Byron swooped down to hunt for my body.

So Byron had been around, no doubt hanging back while Pax and Poe brought me down. He always was a coward.

I saw something splash in the water, Byron said to the others in caw-tongue. He sounded worried. I wasn't sure if he was trying to direct them to give me up for dead, or if he really did think he'd seen me fall into the pond. Either way, I was grateful. I pulled myself as far under the root as I could get, and tried to fold my body up as small as it could go.

They did several low passes through the park, scattering the ducks in their wake. Finally, I heard Pax call out. "You must be right. He's in the water. He's a goner." And then they'd flown away, back to the castle to inform Morchard about my death.

I wasn't dead, but my leg was bleeding quite badly and I knew it was only a matter of time before someone walked past with a big dumb dog off its leash and then I really *would* be a goner. So I'd called out for help, hoping I might be picked up by some well-meaning and dogless citizen.

And of all the people to rescue me, of all the people to have unintentionally involved in this mess, it had to be *her*. The girl from the bakery with the sad eyes and the stunning body and the pale skin that looked so adorable when I made her blush.

She was beautiful, and she was clearly talented. That Heaven & Hell Cake looked like it belonged in the Louvre. But the bakery girl was so shy she couldn't even react to my teasing. She just turned an adorable shade of red and completely shut down. She went for walks in the park by herself. She lived in a flat with no furniture. Something was clearly not right in her life, and she didn't need someone like me hanging around. She didn't need to be brought into my world, especially not now when it was so dangerous.

As much as I might need someone like her.

I gobbled up the last of the peanut butter, and started on the apple. I was lucky that in Bran form I didn't need as much food to give me energy as in human form. I was going to need all the energy I could get just to keep moving through the pain.

The desire to stay and find out more about the mysterious bakery girl was overwhelming. But I had to get out of here, for *her* sake. She looked as if she couldn't deal with any more tragedy in her life, and I would bring her nothing but woe.

I have to leave, and I have to do it now. Because if I see her again, I'm going to stay. And that would be very, very bad. And not just because she was planning to take me to a vet.

I closed my eyes, and started to change.

5

BELINDA

I awoke to a heavy thud in the living room. At first, I thought it must have been Chairman Meow knocking over the dishes I had precariously stacked beside the sink. But then I remembered Chairman Meow was still locked in my room, and I became aware of his heavy, snoring lump pressed against my leg.

Then I remembered the raven. *Maybe he's knocked over the box, or he'd flown out somehow and set about breaking every last thing I owned.* And since I barely owned anything now, I wanted to keep what little I did have intact. I swung my feet out of bed and groggily felt around for the light switch.

As I reached for the door handle, I heard a man curse.

My blood turned cold. There was someone else inside my apartment. I distinctly remembered locking the shop door before I'd gone to bed. The only way up to the apartment was the stairs at the back of the kitchen, unless you scaled the wall and had come in the bathroom window, which would be impossible unless you were Spiderman.

So how had this guy got in? And what did he want?

The last thing I needed was a break-in, but if this supervillain was just after money, why had he come up to the flat? One look at my shabby junk shop couch and chipped dishes and he would head across the road to rob the Kwik-e-Mart. Kwik-e-Mart owners were always rich.

Now I could hear someone moving around.

Fear paralysed me. My hand trembled against the handle. What if he wasn't here for money? What if he knew I was a woman, living alone above a shop, on a street where hardly anyone else would be after dark? What if he had some other purpose in mind?

What should I do? My days as a Girl Guide hadn't prepared me for this. *I know, I'll call the police.* I kept my phone by my bed. As quietly as possible, I tiptoed back toward my dresser—

—My foot caught on the Chairman's belly. He howled in protest as I tumbled forward, flinging my hands out to save my fall. I landed heavily against the stack of plastic tubs I'd been using as a dresser, knocking my phone and several empty tea cups off in the process. These clattered against the floor, and the Chairman dodged through the raining ceramics, meowing at the top of his lungs that he'd just hopped down to help me investigate, and that was no reason to pelt him with crockery.

In the other room, the noise completely stopped.

Shit.

The intruder knew I was awake. If he heard me on the phone, I'd be one dead baker. I couldn't call the police now. All that separated me from the assailant who could be carrying any of a number of terrible weapons was the flimsy door of my bedroom. A door I couldn't even lock.

I was trapped. The only exit out of the flat was in the other room. My bedroom had a single, narrow window, high on the wall, and even if I could loosen the ancient sash wide enough to fit through, it was a two-storey drop down to the street below. There was no conveniently-placed cart of straw or shop awning to save my fall, like there always was in the films.

If I waited for him to enter the bedroom, I'd be screwed. There was nowhere for me to hide. However, the living room had a few more obstacles – the couch, the sacks of flour, the cat trees. Instead of standing here like a frozen target, I'd be better to take my chances in the room beyond, hope that I can duck around him, maybe trip him up with a cat tree, and escape down the stairs before he caught me. It was a stupid plan, but it was the only plan I had. I hoped he didn't have an accomplice waiting down in the shop.

I glanced around my room, hunting for something I could use as a weapon. My eyes fell on my umbrella propped up in the corner of the room. It wasn't much, but it would have to do. I grabbed it, lifted it above my head, and gripped the door handle with a trembling hand.

It was now or never. I took a deep breath, and raised the umbrella behind my head, ready to strike. I pushed open the door.

The man was hunched over the couch, standing on one of the cushions and crouched down as if he were playing leap frog. He stared down at the box I'd been using to hold the raven, the cardboard now crushed and torn in large pieces that were strewn across the floor. My standing lamp had been overturned, and I could see long, jagged tears along the upholstery of the couch. The place looked as if a wild animal had been loose inside.

Which I guess was exactly what had happened. This man didn't seem to be a typical intruder, the kind you saw on crime shows with shifty eyes and a black hoodie. For starters, he appeared to be naked, his dark skin criss-crossed with intricate tattoos. His shoulders bulged with muscles, and his chest was sculpted like a male model. His face was obscured by a mane of long black hair, curling into ringlets at the ends. As he turned toward me, his piercing eyes met mine.

"You?" I cried in disbelief as I recognised him. It was the man from the bakery, the hot biker bad boy who'd flirted with me and bought the Heaven & Hell cake. The man that didn't ask me out, but who had been playing on my mind ever since I'd laid eyes on him. Of all the people I expected to find in my flat, he was not one of them.

He opened his mouth to speak, but all that came out was a strange croak. He looked lost, confused, as if he desperately wanted to explain something but didn't know where to begin.

"Is this what all the flirting was about?" I snapped, inching my way into the room and along the wall, trying to close the distance between myself and the door. "You were distracting me while you cased the joint? Looking for where I hid my safe? My big flour sacks with dollar signs painted on them?"

"While I was ... casing the joint?" The naked biker finally found his voice, and it was still that deep, gravelly, incredibly sexy voice, although now it was dripping with confusion. He held up his hands, showing that he wasn't carrying a weapon. And I couldn't see a knife or gun strapped to his, ah, naked body. "Um ... I know this looks bad, but I can explain—"

Chairman Meow chose that exact moment to shoot out between my two legs, leap up on to the arm of the couch, pull back his ears and hiss at the stranger. The cat's back arched and his fur fluffed up as if he'd stuck his tail into a power outlet. I'd never seen him look like that before.

"Woah!" The man held up his hands as the Chairman swiped at his wrist with his claws. "Easy there, boy!"

"Don't touch him!" I cried out, terrified this guy might be some kind of deranged cat killer.

"I won't, I won't, I'm sorry." The guy slid back along the couch. As he did this, his legs moved and I got quite an eyeful of ... everything. And there was quite a lot of it to eye. He was the most well-endowed criminal I'd ever encountered, and I'd had more than the usual exposure to criminal types.

"Just ... stay there and don't move." I jerked the end of my umbrella in his direction, as I moved closer to the stairs. "I won't call the police or anything, I'd just appreciate it if you left."

"You know, you make one hell of a cake. I haven't been able to get you ... I mean, it ... off my mind all day." He flashed me that heart-melting, devil-may-care smile. But this time, I didn't find it sexy, I found it terrifying. Had he been following me, waiting under the window until he saw the lights go out? "Look, I'm not here to hurt you. You weren't even supposed to see me like this. It's all a bit of a mistake—"

"Are you here to rape me?" I asked, startled by the crassness of my question. "Because just so you know, I intend to put up a fight. I know karate."

I didn't, but he didn't have to know that. People thought all Asians knew karate, and I was happy to play on the stereotype if it would save my ass.

His eyes flashed. "Of course not. I'd never touch you, unless you wanted me to."

"Hey, *you* can't get offended. You're the one sitting naked in my apartment in the middle of the night." Suddenly, realisation dawned. I groaned. How could I have been so stupid not to see it? "Let me guess, you're high, right? You have the munchies and you thought you'd break in and try to steal some pastries? You needed money to pay for your next hit? Well, you're going to be very disappointed when you open the till."

"That's not it." The man held out both hands, palms up. "Please, I can explain. Just stop talking for a second so I can get the words out."

"Fine, but you'd better start explaining." I adjusted my grip on the umbrella. "Or I'll start swinging."

"And you know karate, right?" The man shot me that adorable grin. "Is that an umbrella? What were you going to do, poke me to death?"

"Look, you're the one who broke into my house, so if you're

going to mock my choice of defensive weapon, you can bloody well pack up and leave.'"

"I didn't break in," he said simply. "You brought me here. And now I *can't* leave, because I need your help, and also because I'm not wearing pants."

I snorted. "Excuse me? You came in here because you want *my* help? You're not making any sense."

"You went to the park today, after you closed your shop." He stood up, gripping the edge of the couch as if he were struggling to stand. It was then that I noticed a long, bloody gash across his thigh. The wound looked clean, as though it had been done hours ago, but ugly. No wonder he was struggling to stand up.

He winced as he touched the black ring around his index finger, then turned to face me completely, steadying himself on the kitchen bench, giving me a full view of his sculpted body. Across his chest, arms, thighs and back were stunning tattoos, the most beautiful of which was a black raven in flight across his chest, the wings unfurled and the head pointing to the heavens. I gulped, then nodded, trying not to let my gaze wander from his face. "You picked up an injured raven, and brought it back here. You talked to it, gave it food, and kept it safe from *that* monster," he glared at the Chairman, who was now curled up in the corner, licking his bottom. "Am I right so far?"

"So you *were* stalking me?"

"No. I am that injured raven."

I snorted. What an absurd thing to say. He was clearly a grown man. A grown, naked, tattooed hot, delusional man. He was mentally unstable. He was dangerous.

"It's true. I know it sounds insane, but you have to believe me. It's how I know you love peanut butter, but your last boyfriend was allergic to nuts."

I thought about what he'd said. The broken cage, the way he seemed to know all the things I'd said to the bird, when there was no one else close by. The raven had a damaged leg, and this man had a nasty wound on the same leg. The fact that the raven wasn't anywhere to be seen ...

"I don't believe you," I said, but my words came out sounding more unsure than I'd intended.

'What other explanation is there?" Hot Biker gave me a tentative grin. "Can we just skip past the bit where I explain everything in detail for now? I need you to put down the umbrella and listen to me."

"Yeah right. I put this down and you ravish me."

"For the last time, I would never." He grinned. "Unless you like being ravished. I know I'd enjoy it very much."

My heart hammered against my chest. Goddamn, that grin was intoxicating. I leaned the umbrella up against the wall, and took a small step away from it, making sure I could still lean over and reach it if I needed. "There," I said. "Now, could you sit down, and cover yourself with something. I need to focus."

"Ah, so you *were* looking." He looked relieved as he plopped down on the sofa, and used a cushion to cover his crotch.

I wanted to deny it, but I figured there was no use. My head felt dizzy. I couldn't believe I was even entertaining listening to what this guy had to say. It was that smile, it made me do things I wouldn't normally do. *I bet it made a lot of women do things they wouldn't normally do for that smile.* "Just explain to me what all this is about, and explain carefully, because I have had a long day and I am very tired."

"My name is Cole Erikson, and I am a Bran," he said. "That is a shapeshifter: a human that can turn into a raven. We're a very old species, maybe even older than humans, although our numbers are dwindling now. For centuries we've lived in secret in England, bound to stay here to protect the Empire. For a Bran is not a free creature: he or she is born a servant in a powerful family. Our duty is to spy for our masters, to patrol their land, to deliver messages, to send warnings, and upon their death, to facilitate the journey of their souls into the underworld."

I remembered a visit to the Tower of London when I was much younger with my mother. She and I sat in the courtyard and fed the ravens bread from our ham sandwiches. One of the guides had told me that if the tower ravens were to be lost or fly away, then the Crown would fall, and Britain along with it. At the time I thought it was just a story they told tourists, but listening to Cole, I wasn't so sure.

"Which family do you belong to?" I asked, wondering if he had royal connections. Maybe if I helped him, he could get the Queen to wipe all my debt. Now that would almost compel me to forgive him for the home invasion.

"The Morchards," he answered. "The oldest and richest noble family in Loamshire County. They live on the Morchard Estate, about twenty miles northeast of the village."

"I know that place," I said. "We used to go on school trips to look at the castle. They have a whole wing set up with medieval scenes and wax figures from Madame Tussauds. And there's a—"

"—trebuchet in the courtyard. I know," Cole sighed. "Victor Morchard is quite fond of his family's brutal past. He can trace his family history back to the Norman kings. They've held that castle in their possession since the tenth century. There's some fine examples of gargoyles carved by French artists—"

"You didn't strike me as an architecture buff."

"It's part of the business," Cole said. "When you're a raven, you spend a lot of time perching on things. You tend to develop a bit of snobbery about architraves and gargoyles."

"I see. So let's say I believe that you're a man who can change into a bird, why do you need my help?"

Cole pointed to his leg. "I thought it was obvious. I can't go back there. I need a place to crash, and they wouldn't think to look for me here."

"Wait, what?"

He held up his hand, showing me the black ring. I peered closer, and noticed the skin around the ring was red and inflamed. I reached out to touch it, but Cole snapped his hand away.

"If you touch it, Morchard may be able to track you down. Besides," he winced again. "It's very hot."

"It's burning you?" He nodded miserably. "But why? That's barbaric."

"The ring is a bond. It ties me to my master. I am Victor Morchard's slave, and he uses this ring to control me. Right now I am far from where I should be, I am not performing my duties, and so the ring punishes me."

"Can your master also track you through the ring?" I looked toward the door, wondering what would happen to me if Cole's master suddenly barged in and found his servant naked on my sofa.

Thankfully, Cole was shaking his head. "This is ancient magic, and it's not that sophisticated. I've never been allowed a mobile phone, so Morchard can't trace me here through GPS. He's always trusted that my fear of the pain would keep me in line, and so far it's worked, until today."

He didn't have a mobile phone. So he could never have given me his number, even if he'd wanted to. For some reason, that information made my stomach flutter. "So how did you end up in the park?"

"I had enough. I was trying to escape from the castle, but my master's other Bran found me, and did this." Cole rubbed the wound on his leg, wincing as his fingers touched the sensitive skin. "If a Bran goes rogue, as I have done, we're trained to kill it, in order to preserve the family's secrets. Bran know a lot of secrets."

"I can imagine. So you were hiding from them under that tree. And then I picked you up?"

Cole nodded. "And a good thing, too. The cut was pretty bad. I could barely move. The first dog walking through the park would have finished me off. But, I also knew it was dangerous being with you. That's why I leapt out at the crossing. But I didn't figure on you being completely crazy and chasing me through the traffic like that."

I blushed, remembering the cars zooming around me and all the honking and name calling and rude hand gestures. I'd never done anything like that before in my life. Just the thought of running out into that traffic after the silly bird made my cheeks burn.

"And you brought me back here and cleaned me up and gave me something to eat." Cole's deep voice dripped with gratitude. "You were so kind. No one has ever done anything like that for me before. But I'm a danger to you. I didn't want you to get involved. I wanted to keep you safe, so I was just going to sneak out of here while you were asleep, find some clothes, and go into hiding. But then you woke up."

"Yes."

He shrugged. "So I can't hide anymore. You know what I am. That means you're involved, whether you like it or not. And I was hoping, since there's nothing I can do about that now, maybe I could appeal to some of that kindness you've already shown me, and ask you to help me."

"What help could you possibly need from *me?*"

"Well, for starters, I could do with some clothes."

"I'm afraid I might not be much help in that department," I said, gesturing to my own tiny frame. "I'm not sure anything I own will be able to fit you."

"You sure do know how to flatter a guy's ego." Cole grinned. "Anything is fine, really. Mostly, I could do with a place to crash for a couple of days, until I can figure out what to do. There's someone in Crookshollow I need to see before I leave."

"A girl?"

Cole tilted his head to the side and grinned at me. "No. Why, are you jealous?"

"Hardly."

"So what about it? Will you let me stay? I promise I won't get in your way. I just need to see this person – this *male* person –and then I'll be going."

"Um ..." I paused. *Why are you even entertaining this? He's a naked biker dude covered in tattoos who probably has a drug problem, and he's just fed you this cockamamie story about being a shapeshifting raven, and you're thinking about letting him say in your house?* "Yeah, sure. You can stay."

Apparently, I had a weak spot for naked biker corvids.

Cole's whole face lit up. "You have no idea what this means, seriously. It's incredible. I will repay you, somehow."

I looked away, my cheeks flushing with colour as I imagined one way he might repay me. Damnit, why did I have to turn into such a mess around this guy?

Cole's husky voice reverberated through my body. "From the looks of your red cheeks, you've already thought of a way. I'll be right here if you ever want to tell me about it ..."

My blush deepened. I glanced at the microwave clock. It read 2:15AM. I had to get up in an hour and fifteen minutes. "I'm too tired to think about any more of this tonight," I said, and as the words left my mouth, I knew it was true. Weariness crawled through my limbs, and my whole body felt heavy. Suddenly, nothing sounded better than crawling back into bed and consigning myself to a deep sleep.

"Of course." Cole nodded, serious again. "We should both sleep, Nightingale. I can tell you more in the morning."

"Nightingale?"

"After Florence Nightingale," he grinned, pointing at his leg. "She used to nurse soldiers back to health during the Crimean War. Many a soldier found her sweet voice their only solace."

"Oh," I felt my cheeks reddening again. "Er ... thanks."

"Well, you haven't told me your name yet, so I had to make one up."

"Oh," I stared at the floor, not wanting to meet those devilish eyes again. "It's Belinda. Belinda Wu."

"Belinda," he rolled my name over his tongue in a way that made me wish he were screaming it in ecstasy. "You are an angel, you know that?"

I'm a pushover, is what I am. I found an old, threadbare blanket at the back of my closet (evidently, Ethan hadn't thought it worth stealing), and Cole piled up a couple of cushions to use as a pillow. I offered him an old t-shirt of Ethan's to wear, but when he tried to pull it over his head, it tore across his broad shoulders. "Don't worry about it," he grinned, tossing the scraps of fabric into the corner. "I'll just sleep naked."

I gulped. With only my thin bedroom wall separating me from hot, naked Cole, how was I *ever* going to get any sleep?

AS I SUSPECTED, after turning out the lights and flopping my weary body back into bed, I found that I now couldn't sleep. I lay on top of the blankets, my eyes squeezed shut, but my ears tingling as I listened in the darkness for the sounds of Cole breathing heavily.

I couldn't believe he was here, in *my* flat. He was the first guy who had ever seen my shabby upstairs rooms, once storage and an office for the shop, but now the only accommodation I could afford. In fact, he was the first person *ever* – with the exception of Chairman Meow – who had seen the full expanse of what Ethan had left me with.

What did he think of me, this mousy asian girl with the bare, cold flat who had rescued him? Probably not much. He may be in trouble now, but he had a life that was filled with magic and intrigue and probably hot raven shapeshifter chicks. I must seem boring beyond belief to him, and he hadn't even experienced my fourteen-hour work days—

Hang on a second.

As my mobile phone buzzed to life, signalling that it was time to get up and bake bread, an idea floated into my sleep-deprived brain. It was a crazy idea, one that I could only consider after hours of wakefulness and the newfound knowledge that human/animal shapeshifters actually existed. I turned it over and over in my mind, searching for flaws, but I couldn't find any. Cole had a problem, I had a problem, and this crazy idea would solve both.

Don't do it. A voice inside my head warned. *Don't get involved. He's clearly running from something. Think of how scary something has to be to make a guy that strong run away? You only want to help him because it will keep him near you a little longer, and you're lonely and desperate and thinking that if only you could find a man like James Bond—*

Shut up, I commanded. For once, the voice obeyed.

I got up and tiptoed through to the kitchen, past a snoring Cole. He had rolled on to his side, facing the back of the couch, the blanket balled up under his arms, revealing his muscular back and tight, toned arse. Intricate tattoos covered every inch of it, and I thought I even recognised Bianca's handiwork on the carefully rendered skeletal wings that swept down his back. A second raven sat on top of a grinning skull on one cheek, and the bird bent down to fish around in the eye socket. My fingers itched to touch his skin, to run my hands over the ink.

That's enough of that. I tore my eyes away. *No more drooling over the hot naked Bran on your couch. You have a job to do, and so does he.* I grabbed a pot and wooden spoon from the stack by the sink, stood over the couch, and clanged the top of the pot with the spoon.

CLANG CLANG CLANG.

"What the fuck are you doing?" Cole yelled, scrambling away from me. The blanket caught beneath him, and he toppled off the couch, landing in a heap on the floor. He scrambled to sit up again and untangle his body from the blankets.

"It's time to get up."

"The sun isn't even in the fucking sky yet!"

"Ah, yes, but that means there's still a couple of hours before my first customer walks in the door." I explained, grinning despite myself. This was a completely cheeky, very un-Belinda-like idea. I couldn't believe I was doing it. "I've decided that I'm happy to help you, and you're welcome to stay here as long as you need to. But I am not a homeless bird shelter. You don't get this hospitality for nothing."

"You call this hospitality?" Cole growled, holding his hands over his ears. I grinned and clanged the pot a few more times.

"If you're staying here, you need to pull your weight."

"Excuse me?"

"You heard me. Take your hands off your ears and put some clothes on. I need you downstairs. You have some bread to knead."

"I don't have any clothes, and I don't knead bread." He folded his arms. "I've never baked anything before. I'm really more of a messenger, and a ferrier of souls to the underworld. If you need any messages delivered or souls ferried …"

"I use email for messages, and I'm fresh out of souls for the time being," I said, studying his face to see how serious he was about the soul thing. That didn't sound like something I wanted to know about. "And don't worry. I have an assistant who doesn't know how to bake anything, either. In fact, I can already tell you'll be a big improvement over him, on account that you have at least successfully held down a job." *And you're not too bad to look at,* I added silently.

Cole laughed, a little uneasily. "You are serious, aren't you? You actually want me to help you in the bakery?"

"Why not? It's not as if your master is going to think to look for you here." I pointed to the bathroom. "Go have a shower, and

I'll find you some clothes. I assume you don't want me to take you to the vet after all?"

Cole met my eyes with an intense gaze. For a moment I thought he was going to refuse. But then he sighed and stood up, wincing as he tried to put weight on his leg. "We can skip the vet visit. And you're right. I owe you for fixing me up and letting me hide out here. But don't say I didn't warn you."

6

COLE

You are a fuck up.

Not only did you not manage to sneak out of here, but now she's involved up to her pretty little ears. It's not just about saving your own arse anymore, you've got Belinda to think about.

Beautiful Belinda Wu, who claimed to know martial arts but didn't look as though she could stand to squash a spider. She checked over my leg again, sprayed it with some antiseptic, and gave me a roll of sandwich wrap to keep it dry in the shower. I watched her shuffle out of the room, her cute ass wiggling in her shorts as she loped down the stairs. She was unusually vigorous for someone who'd been woken up only two hours previously by a raven turning into a man, and then having her 3:30AM alarm go off, and she hadn't had any coffee yet. I guessed the life of a baker really only suited morning people.

Belinda was clearly one of those women who had no idea how attractive she was. She hid behind a curtain of black hair, and could barely look at me when I was sitting there naked. When she was tending my wound she would only look directly at my leg. But I could see she was curious. Perhaps it was my ink, I wondered if she'd ever been with a guy who had tatts before. Somehow I doubted it.

I knew what Belinda saw when she looked at me - the kind of guy her mother warned her about, the kind that racked up criminal misdemeanours the way other men collected hedge funds. The bad boy who would rock her world and leave her heartbroken.

She probably wasn't wrong.

As much as I wanted to throw her up against the wall and fuck her brains out, that wasn't what she needed. Whatever had happened to her, one thing was clear: she'd been hurt real bad, and she was still recovering. She didn't need me making things worse for her just because I found her so fucking adorable.

I needed to exercise some self-control. I'd already broken my number one rule with her – don't get attached. You can't fall in love until you are free – and I hadn't even fucked her yet.

And you won't. I scolded myself before I could put that delectable thought into action. I was currently running for my life, I couldn't afford to get distracted. And from the looks of her empty flat, she *really* couldn't afford to have me distract her. For once, I needed to stop thinking with my cock and think with my head.

But she was so damn cute. If I could manage to get through a day without pouncing on her, it would be a miracle in the order of loaves and fishes.

I lifted my armpits and sniffed. Yuck. I smelled like blood and sweat and wet grass and peanut butter. I walked into the small bathroom and turned the shower on, fiddling with the temperamental taps until I got a good, hot blast. I stood under the water and let the hot stream pummel my skin, and I tried desperately hard to ignore my cock, which had stiffened at the memory of Belinda's reddening face and cute arse sliding around in those shorts.

This was going to be an interesting couple of days.

The ring on my finger tightened, sending a sharp stab of pain down my side, instantly obliterating any amorous thoughts. The pain was getting worse the longer I stayed away. In a couple of days it would be unbearable, which might not matter, because on Sunday, the bond between myself and Morchard would be severed, and a new bond would form with Sir Thomas Gillespie. I would be bound to my father's murderer, unless I could find a way to rid myself of the curse.

I have to talk to Mikael.

One thing was working in my favour. I was now hiding out only a few doors down from the pub where he worked, and although Victor probably knew I was alive (for he'd still be picking up the signature of my ring), he would assume I was far away by now. They were probably looking for me in Yorkshire by now.

I hoped like hell news of my death had reached Thomas Gillespie. Then, at least Victor would have more problems to deal with than a Bran that ran away. Gillespie wouldn't take kindly to being informed he had purchased a Bran that had gone AWOL, especially as Victor had probably spent all his money by now. I would have to get Mikael to make inquiries for me, but either way, I would probably be fine here in Crookshollow for a few days, until I could figure out my next move.

Besides, I told myself as I rinsed off. *I need to stay here to protect Belinda. I couldn't just leave her on her own before I made sure Pax and Poe wouldn't come after her for any reason.*

She asked me to stay. She needed me. She said so. I was doing a good thing by being here.

Wasn't I?

7

BELINDA

*J*ust around the corner from *Bewitching Bites* was a charity shop. Outside is a bin where you could toss old clothes you don't want any more, which they either tried to sell or took along to a homeless shelter. I'd never really owned many clothes anyway, and Ethan had taken most of my nice items (Why? I don't know. Maybe he thought he could sell them. Maybe he was fueling his secret cross-dressing fetish. Maybe he just wanted to completely screw me over.) so for the last few months I'd been raiding this particular bin every time I needed something new. I'd even nicked off with some dish towels and a tablecloth. I felt pretty awful about it, because I was in essence stealing from the poor, but I was pretty bloody poor myself. I hoped it wasn't a hanging offense.

A quick rummage around revealed an old Iron Maiden t-shirt with a massive hole under the armpit, and a pair of black trousers with some strange stains on the knee. Both looked as if they might fit Cole. I grabbed my booty and rushed back up to my shop. When I got upstairs, I heard the water running in the shower, and Chairman Meow was prowling around the bathroom door.

"Cole!" I called out, picking up the cat. He sniffed the clothes, made a disgusted face, and nuzzled my chin.

"Your soap smells like unicorn farts." Cole yelled through the door.

"If only I'd known that earlier, I would've bottled it and made my fortune. I'm putting some clothes outside the door," I dumped the pants and shirt in a pile. "Put them on and meet me downstairs when you're done."

I went down to the bakery and fired up the ovens. As the room heated up, I took off my sweater, so I was working in just a threadbare white tank top and some unflattering men's shorts. I put a hairnet on and got to work mixing the dough for the bread into the large, old-fashioned mixer. I'd brought the thing on eBay when the bakery first opened for a steal, thinking that I'd be able to afford to replace it with something new and shiny by the end of the first year. The great cosmic mixer joke was on me. I was stuck with the ancient mixer for the rest of my life.

Cole sauntered down the stairs, one hand holding up the pants, the other running through his wet hair. He winced a little as he stood on his injured leg. In the light, the black stubble on his chin and cheeks stood out even more. He looked rugged, dangerous. And he smelled like my soap. God, he was sexy. How was I going to survive being in the tiny kitchen with him?

"These are way too big," he growled, pulling at the clothes. "And they smell like feet."

"Hey, naked raven beggars can't be choosers. As soon as the shops open, I'll go out and buy you some real clothes." I pointed to one of the bags of flour that were standing beside the mixer. "Open one of those, dump the flour in the mixer, and you can use the cord to tie up your pants."

"I look like an idiot."

"No, you look like a metalhead who's just had his wallet stolen. But there's only one person who's going to see you back here, and that's me. And I happen to think that t-shirt is an improvement. Now, first things first." I waved a hairnet under his nose. "You can't do anything in here without one of these."

Surprisingly, Cole obeyed, tugging the net over his long tresses and pulling the elastic tight. Strangely, he managed to look even hotter with his hair off his face. His sharp cheekbones and piercing eyes stood out. "What next?" He grinned.

I explained to him how to make the bread, and then pulled one of last night's cakes out of the fridge and started making chocolate ganache. Cole had to slip past me in the narrow kitchen in order to get to the mixer. I watched him out of the corner of my eye, telling myself I needed to make sure he did things properly, but knowing secretly that I was perving at the way his shoulders bulged as he picked up that heavy flour sack as if it were a pillowcase. As he tore open the sack and leaned over the mixer to dump the flour inside, his pants slipped down his hips, revealing a stripe of his bare butt and the edge of that raven and skull tattoo. I felt my cheeks redden, but I couldn't turn away.

Cole whirled around, dropping the empty sack and grabbing his pants. "Are you sure you want me to use this?" He held up the string from the sack as he leaned on his good leg. "You were looking mighty pleased with the view only a few minutes ago."

I turned away, my cheeks burning. *I can't believe he saw me.* "You're disgusting. This is a *kitchen*."

"You love it."

"Make sure you wash your hands after touching yourself like that." I yelled over my shoulder.

"As you wish." Cole slid back behind me to get to the sink, his body grazing mine, making tiny bumps appear across my skin. As he moved past me, he pinched my arse. My whole body shuddered at his touch. *What is with me today? At this rate we're never going to get the bread ready.*

"What next?" Cole grinned.

"Add that yeast, and twenty-two litres of water. Then turn the mixer on. You'll need to mix it for about ten minutes, and watch it to make sure all the flour on the sides gets scraped in. After that, call me over and I'll show you how to knead it."

He gave me a salute. "Aye, aye, Captain!"

I tore my gaze away from Cole and forced myself to focus on the cakes and slices. As I carefully drizzled melted chocolate over the caramel squares, I heard pots crashing and Cole swearing behind me. *I will not look,* I told myself. As fun as Cole was, the clock was ticking and I had to get everything done, or I wouldn't make rent.

I heard the mixer flick on, and listened to the familiar *THWACK THWACK* as the dough came together and bounced against the sides of the bowl. I slid the caramel squares into the fridge to set, and went to work on the carrot cake and the lemon scones.

"All done." Cole called out behind me. I heard the mixer shut off and whir in protest as it wound down. I turned around, and almost choked.

Cole looked like a ghost. His entire body, from his head to his feet, was coated in white flour. There was also flour all over the mixer, across the benches, over the stacks of pans and pots, and in a giant arc across the floor.

"There was an ... incident." He grinned. "But I'm on top of it."

The weird thing was, if Finn had done the same thing, (which he had on numerous occasions, the ancient mixer could be a bit temperamental), I would have lost my shit. But Cole standing there trying to look tough while completely coated in flour, made a giggle rise up inside me. I tried to hold it in, but that only made me want to laugh harder. I clamped my hands over my mouth, just as a great snort-laugh escaped between my fingers.

"Don't laugh at me," Cole growled, and his tone was so serious that it only made me laugh harder. I fell against the bench, gasping for breath as I clutched my stomach. I bent over, laughing so hard that tears sprung in my eyes and my breath came out in a giant wheeze.

"That's it, if you think this is funny, then you try looking like an abominable snowman." Cole grabbed a handful of flour from the open sack on the bench and lobbed it at me. But flour, of course, doesn't stick together like snow. A giant cloud of white puffed out across the kitchen, coating Cole and the benches and floor, while miraculously managing to completely miss me.

"Nice try, Casper." I dodged out of the way as Cole lunged at me. With his injured leg, he was slow enough that I managed to duck around him. But now my back was pressed against the bench at one end of the kitchen. There was no where else for me to go. Cole grinned as he shoved his hand in the bag again and drew out another fistful of flour.

"Come back here, Belinda. Come back here so I can give you a big hug!" Cole held his arms out wide and dived at me. I yelped and ducked, trying to go under him, but he used his good leg to trap me. He threw his arms around me and lifted me off the ground, his warm body enveloping mine in an enormous bear hug. Or bird hug.

"Argh, stop it!" I yelped, as Cole reached up and rubbed the flour through my hairnet, smearing it all down my cheeks and over my shoulders. As I reached up to slap him away, he grabbed me under the arms and picked me up, pushing me back so I was sitting on the bench, legs open around him, our faces just inches apart.

All thoughts of struggling fled from my mind, along with the voice that was screaming at me that this was a bad idea. I became aware of just how close we were, my breasts were nearly touching his chest, his crotch was only an inch from mine. All I could see, all I could *feel*, was Cole, the warmth of his body, his eyes boring into mine ...

"Hey," he whispered, his voice hoarse. His lips dangerously close to mine. His breath tickled my skin.

"Hey," I whispered back. My heart hammered against my chest. The blood rushed in my ears. *Please, kiss me ...*

I heard a crash behind me. Cole leapt back, and I bit my lip and jumped so high my head hit the shelf above and knocked off a stack of cake pans. They clattered against the flour-covered floor. The door to the kitchen slammed back against its hinges. I looked up, my heart pounding and the taste of blood in my mouth.

Thankfully, it wasn't the health inspector. It was only Finn, arriving to work 45 minutes late, of course.

"This place is insane. What did you do? You always yell at me when I make a mess," he pouted.

"Yeah," I gasped, holding my chest as my heart rate returned to normal. I slid off the bench and tried in vain to dust off the front of my shirt. My face hurt from all the blushing. "I do."

"Hey, who's that?" Finn jabbed an accusatory finger at Cole.

"He's ... your replacement," I said, another wild idea suddenly occurred to me.

"What the fuck?"

"Hey, watch your language around a lady," Cole piped up, his muscular arms crossed over his white body.

"I'm sorry, Finn." As I said the words, I realised they were a lie. I wasn't sorry at all. A rush of relief flooded through me. I'd been so desperate for the help that I'd kept Finn on for weeks and weeks, but all his presence did was stress me out. And having Cole here made me realise that I didn't need Finn, he was only making things worse. I would find a way to manage, somehow.

"You can't just replace me." Finn snapped. "My stepfather is a lawyer. He'll be on your arse so fast you'll never sell another Eccles cake again."

That made me shudder. I had heard Finn tell stories about his stepfather, and how he took great pride in crushing his opponents. I couldn't afford to be crushed. *Maybe I've made a huge mistake—*

Cole stepped forward, his body lurching slightly as he put weight on his injured leg. His bulky frame towered over Finn, his broad shoulders nearly as wide as the doorframe. "Are you threatening Belinda, you little punk?"

Finn gave a little squeak.

Cole grabbed Finn by the collar and pulled him up, slamming his back against the wall. Finn's face had gone bone white. "Listen to me very carefully," Cole said, his voice calm, conversational, as if he were discussing the latest cricket match. He leaned right in close, so their noses were practically touching. "This bakery is Belinda's life, and for some reason, she gave your little punk arse a chance. You show up late, and you have no aptitude for baking. So she's well within her rights to get rid of you. I would have had you out on the street on the first day if you behaved like that, but Belinda is too nice, so she lets you stay and keeps paying you even though you're worth sweet fanny adams to her bottom line. And now, you want to take her to court for finally wising up? If anything, she should be the one suing *you*. But you're lucky, because this new arrangement works out well for you. Now you don't have to get up at 4AM in the morning, and you get to go back to planning dairy robberies or beat boxing or whatever it is you do with your sorry life. This is a win-win, got it? And don't let my rakish charms fool you, I'm pretty well connected in this town. I have friends who could make your life hell. So we're done here, aren't we?"

Finn nodded vigorously. Cole let him down. With a terrified glance over at me, Finn turned on his heel and bolted from the shop as fast as his scrawny legs could carry him.

As soon as he'd gone, the reality of what I'd done hit me. Finn was the last of my staff, he may have been useless, but at least with him around, I could take the occasional break. Without him, I was completely on my own. I was already working 80 hour weeks, and it still wasn't enough to get everything done. My legs felt wobbly, my resolve crumbling around me like an overcooked Victoria sponge. I slumped down, leaning my back against the cool metal of the mixer, and buried my face in my hands.

"You don't need him," Cole said from the doorway.

"I kind of do, though." I mumbled through my fingers. "I have to do it all on my own. I can't do it, it's too much."

My whole body shook. A lump rose in my throat. Any second now I was going to start crying, and then it was over. I was going to start crying, and it was going to be one of those big, painful cries that comes from your belly and makes your face splotchy and snot pour from every orifice. And the last thing I wanted to do was break down like that in front of Cole. I sucked in a deep breath, and then another. *Please, keep it together. Just excuse yourself and run upstairs—*

"Nightingale, what's wrong?"

Fuck. I was gone. My tears spilled over and my whole body juddered with the force of my sob. I jammed my palms into my eyes and cried as silently as I could into them, feeling the tears and the snot run down my face and mingle with the flour, creating a gluggy, sticky mess. *And to think a few moments ago I was hoping this guy would kiss me. Not a chance now. I really am a hot mess.*

Why can't I do anything right? Why do I have to fail at everything? Why can't I make this work on my own?

Cole slid down beside me. Rough hands grabbed my wrists and prised them away from my eyes. I turned away from him, not wanting him to see me like this, but he said sternly. "Belinda, look at me."

"I can't. I—" I turned back to him. Cole stared at me with those intense eyes, his face unwavering. He squeezed my wrists.

"I don't know what all this is about, but you don't have to worry. You're not alone. You have me now. I'm a fast learner."

I snorted, blowing snot through my flour-caked nose. "Your rakish good charms aren't much good in here, either, you know. You just coated my entire kitchen in flour. We don't even have the loaves in the oven yet. It's a disaster. It's all falling apart. I'll never get everything done on time."

"Don't you have other staff? I'm sure they could pick up the slack a little—"

"There's no one else!" I sobbed. "I couldn't afford to pay them. I can't even afford to pay you. Hell, I can't even afford all this flour."

Cole grabbed my wrists and pulled my hands off my face. "You're serious?"

I nodded miserably.

"Come here," Cole pulled me close to him. I fought him at first, not wanting to get close when I was such a mess. We tugged against each other for a few moments, but he won, and I collapsed against him. His hands on my back felt strong, reassuring.

"Here's what we're going to do," he said. "We're gonna go upstairs, wash our faces off, and get to work. We're going to get the bread in the oven and whatever else you need, and if anyone complains about it being a few minutes late, then they can answer to me, okay?"

I nodded, not trusting myself to speak.

"I will be here all day, in my beautiful new duds, to do whatever it is you need. And then, after all the work is finished, I am taking you out." I started to protest, but he held a finger over my lips. "No arguments. We're gonna hit the town, you're gonna let your hair down for a night, and then you will tell me why a woman who makes the best goddamned cake I've ever tasted is flat broke. And we will try to figure out a solution, because I bet there is one, but you're just too tired and stressed to see it."

"But ... I don't even know you. Why are you—"

"Right now you know all you need to know about me," Cole said. "I'm the raven. I'll tell you tonight, a secret for a secret, okay?"

I nodded.

"And I know all I need to know about you, Belinda. You're the woman who saves injured birds and refuses to ask anyone for help. That's enough to get us through today, and then, tonight, we can share the rest of our secrets, okay?"

Woah. That was pretty intense. I sucked in a deep breath. "Yeah, that's okay."

~

WITH COLE in the kitchen being sensible, we kneaded the bread and fitted it into the baking pans in record time. By the time I turned the oven on, we were only running fifteen minutes behind schedule. At 5AM my deliveries started to arrive, and Cole unloaded them with ease, lifting the heavy bags of flour and packages of meat as though they were filled with feathers. I was left with more time than usual to do all the finishing work, and I was even able to whip up a special batch of orange and poppy-seed muffins. Cole quickly picked up all the tasks I gave him, and he even suggested we add a little smoked paprika to the Cornish pasties, which gave the whole kitchen a wonderful, rich, spicy aroma.

Out front, I arranged the cakes and slices in the cabinet while Cole flipped over the sign and wiped down the tables. I stood back and admired the empty shop. It was the first time in months I'd actually been able to take a breath and appreciate what I'd created. I loved the *Bewitching Bites* decor, with all the kitschy occult art on the walls and the 80s and 90s board games I had placed on the centres of the tables. I loved the little witch that sat beside the till and the stacks of flyers for local metal bands and poetry readings lined up along the windowsill.

"We did it, Nightingale." Cole whispered in my ear. I blushed at the nickname, all the hairs on my neck standing on end as his breath brushed over them.

"That was almost fun," I said, which was another lie. It *had* been fun. The bakery hadn't been fun in a long time. But now, staring at the cute wooden tables and mismatched vintage chairs, and the glass counter bursting with delicious treats, I actually felt excited again. This was my dream, and even though it was hard now, it was really happening.

I went to teach Cole how to run the coffee machine, but he brushed me off. "I've been making coffee for the Morchards ten times a day since I was a chick," he said. "I know what I'm doing."

I left him to it, wondering how cute he must've been as a little baby raven chick.

At 6:05, my first customer came in, right on time. Douglas Ackerman was a 72-year-old widower who walked his little dog Bettie in the mornings. He always stopped in for a coffee, mince pie, and a Florentine. I usually didn't allow dogs in the store, but Bettie was an exception, as she was tiny and well-behaved and almost as old as Douglas himself.

"Good morning Mr. Ackerman," I greeted him from behind the counter. "I have your usual all ready for you here." Cole handed me the flat white I'd asked him to prepare.

Douglas leaned over the counter and whispered to me conspiratorially. "Who's your handsome fella, Miss Belinda?"

"Oh, he's not my ... I mean ..." The blush crept along my cheeks. "He's my new assistant."

"No more Finn?"

"No more Finn."

"In that case," Mr. Ackerman squinted at the cabinet. "I'll take one of those Cornish pasties. They look particularly delicious today, most likely owing to Master Finn's absence. I can eat it for my lunch."

Grinning despite myself, I bagged up his pasty and rung up his order.

As soon as Mr. Ackerman left, more people started to trickle in, and the trickle turned into a flood as lorry drivers and commuters grabbed a quick breakfast on the way to work. We quickly fell into a routine. Cole would bag the hot food and make the coffee, and I stood behind the counter, served the slices, organised the bread orders, and talked to the customers. Having Cole there gave me this strange sense of confidence, and I found myself chatting brightly to people, asking them about their day, and recommending particular treats. Who was this person? Usually I just smiled awkwardly and handed them their orders while trying to avoid eye contact.

Cole was clearly in his element. He grinned at everyone, and flirted outrageously with the women. I went out for half an hour to choose some clothes for him at the menswear store down the road, and when I returned he had sold another whole Heaven & Hell cake to a smitten single mother. I hope her ten-year old daughter loved the whisky ganache on her birthday cake. The old ladies from the Crookshollow Knit n Bitch came in for their 10AM coffee and ended up staying until 2PM. Mrs. Van Uppity's eyes practically fell out of her head every time Cole refilled her cup.

I felt a tiny surge of jealousy while I watched him flirt with a young blonde lady dressed to kill in a corporate suit and spiked pumps. He could have a woman like her, he didn't want someone like me who always smelled faintly of bread and whose pores were permanently dusted with flour. But, even I had to admit that his sales tactics were working. I'd never seen the sweets counter so empty this early in the day.

After 2:30PM, we hit a bit of a lull before the school run got in. I set Cole on replenishing the depleted cabinet with the last of the stores from the fridge, while I got started on a batch of biscuits for the next day. I looked up from the batter to check the clock on the wall opposite the counter, just as Elinor walked in.

I froze. How was I going to explain Cole? I thought about telling him to hide, but it was too late. Elinor hadn't noticed him yet, but she was walking up to the counter. Any second now she'd see him. She called out to me. "Bianca has just finished two chest pieces back-to-back. She's having a major energy crash. I need 10CCs of triple espresso and a chocolate brownie, stat!"

"Does she want that in tablet form, or just hooked directly to her veins?" Cole asked, poking his head up from behind the glass display.

Elinor's eyes bugged out when she saw who was behind the counter. She stuttered out an answer and Cole went off to prepare the coffee. While the machine was screaming, Elinor pulled me across the counter and hissed in my ear. "That's the arrogant biker guy from yesterday? What is he doing here? He isn't holding you hostage, is he?"

"No." I shifted uncomfortably. I hadn't figured out what I was going to tell her. "Cole is just helping out—"

"Cole? So Arrogant Biker has a name now. You seem awfully friendly with this *Cole* all of a sudden. What happened to Finn?"

"I fired him."

"Belinda Wu, look at you being all sassy and authoritative." Elinor beamed. "I love it. But seriously, why did you hire that guy? He was such a sleaze. I demand to know what's going on."

"It's a ... long story. I haven't actually hired him, he's just helping me out for a few days. But it's a good thing, trust me." I grinned at her. "See? I'm happy."

"I'll say. That's the first genuine smile I've seen on your face in months." Elinor grinned back. "Got anymore hot bikers back there I don't know about?"

"Shut up."

"What about firemen? I love firemen."

"Don't be ridiculous."

"At this rate, you're going to have to rename this place 'Hot Buns'."

"Elinor!"

"Here's your coffee," Cole said, handing the takeaway cup over my head.

"Thank you very much, *Cole*." Elinor gave him a saccharine smile. "We seem to be bumping into each other a lot this week."

"Indeed. It's been a pleasure."

"Well, I best be off. I'll be seeing you tomorrow, Cole." Elinor jabbed me in the arm. "And you have some explaining to do. We'll still be seeing you on Friday?"

"Oh, definitely." Every Friday the girls got together for drinks. I usually couldn't go, because I had too much work to do and a 3:30AM wake-up call the following day, so recently they'd started coming around to the shop with a bottle of wine instead. They sat around and drank while I baked. I looked forward to it all week.

One thing was certain, I had until Friday to come up with some kind of believable reason for Cole's existence in my life. I didn't think the whole, "I rescued a raven from the park and he turned out to be a hot guy," was going to fly.

One problem at a time, Belinda. First, you need to get through your date tonight. Your date with a raven.

FOUR O'CLOCK ROLLED AROUND, and I was almost sorry to put out the CLOSED sign. There were plenty of people outside keen for a pie, but we'd sold out of *everything*, and I needed to start baking if I had any hope of opening the next day.

It wasn't just the high sales that kept the smile on my face. With Cole in the store, I'd had more fun than I had in months. He made me laugh, he put the customers at ease, he wiped down the tables and cabinet without me even having to ask, and every time he accidentally brushed past me or touched my hand, sparks of electricity flew through my body.

After we closed, Cole helped me do some prep for the following day. I showed him how to bake the pastry for the pies and prepare the fillings, and he took charge of that while I whizzed and stirred and boiled and blitzed to prep all ten different slices and cakes for the following day. Even with two of us working, it took hours. With every glimpse at the clock, all possibility of our date that night faded into oblivion. By eight-thirty, even Cole was starting to look tired. "You do all this work, every single day?" He asked me. "When do you have time to have a life?"

"*Bewitching Bites* is my life. At least at the moment. As soon as my debts are paid off, I'll be able to afford to get some staff in to manage the shop, and then I'll just do the baking, and things will be a lot easier."

"When will that be?"

"In about seven years time."

"I really hope you're joking."

"I am not joking. And I really don't want to talk about it."

"Are we done here?' Cole pulled out the last batch of pies and slammed the door on the oven.

"Sure, for now." I wiped a line of chocolate brownie batter off my cheek. "We'll have to do the bread and the final prep tomorrow morning."

"Go upstairs and have a shower," Cole said. "I'll finish cleaning up down here. And then, I'm taking you out."

My stomach flipped. "Are ... are you sure you still want to go out? It's really late."

"That doesn't matter. I haven't forgotten my promise from this morning. Come on, you look as if you could do with eating something that wasn't filled with jam and cream."

His comment stung. I already hated the little stomach I saw when I looked down at my body, the mound of flesh around my belly reminding me that I had been subsisting on a diet of bakery castoffs for months. Cole looked at my face, and realisation dawned on his. "Damnit, sorry, Belinda. I didn't mean that the way it came out. Honestly, I think you look smoking hot. I just meant, perhaps a good steak will buck up your spirits a bit. It usually does for me."

He thinks I look smoking hot? HE THINKS I LOOK SMOKING HOT? I stared down at my shoes, so he wouldn't see the smile plastered across my face or the burn in my cheeks. "Really? I thought ravens were more into carrion and eyeballs."

"A rare steak is almost as good as some fresh carrion." Cole grinned. I screwed up my face in disgust. "Sorry, my brother would've appreciated that joke. You do still want to go? You aren't rethinking our bargain? You tell me your secrets, and I'll tell you mine."

I raced upstairs, leaping over the steps two at a time. I frantically searched through my closet for something, *anything,* suitable for a date with a hot biker raven. I found a long black maxi dress in the back of my closet, one of the only nice items of clothing Ethan hadn't taken from me, since it had been in the wash at the time. I set that out on the bed, along with a red scarf and some black pumps, and went into the bathroom.

In the shower, I dragged a razor over my legs and armpits, wincing as I cut my skin tugging at the thick, curled hair. I'd been so stressed and tired lately that hygiene had gone out the window. I sprayed myself with perfume, hoping it would disguise my permanent bread smell. I wrapped a towel around my body, and pushed open the bathroom door.

Cole was in the living room, grinning at me from the couch. "If you insist on dressing like that, I'm not going to want to take you out. We can just stay right here and ..."

I raced into my room so that he wouldn't notice the fact my whole body was blushing. "You're disgusting." I called out of the closed door.

"You love it, Nightingale." I opened the door a crack and watched as he grabbed his towel from the back of the couch and entered the bathroom, whistling a tune. I leaned against the wall, my heart flipping. When he called me that name, my whole body flushed with pleasure.

By the time I was dressed, my hair combed and pinned, and a light dusting of makeup on my face, Cole had showered and pulled on the pair of tight black jeans, and a black t-shirt that emphasized his broad shoulders and thin waist. Black and grey tattoos curled around his forearms, disappearing beneath the edge of the shirt.

"Whoa, you clean up nice, Nightingale." Cole grinned when he saw me.

"You're not so bad yourself," I grinned back, my heart doing that flipping thing again. "I have great taste in clothes. That shirt looks great on you."

"You should see me with my feathers on."

I set down a bowl of food for Chairman Meow and locked up the shop. Cole leaned against a power pole, keeping his weight on his good leg. "I was thinking we could go to the pub down the road. It's dark there so less chance of anyone seeing me, and we really need to talk without some snooty waiter interrupting us to talk about the wine list. I hope you don't mind."

"I don't mind at all. But Cole, I don't have a lot of money and your clothes kind of wiped me out—"

"Hey, I asked you out, remember? Don't worry, I've got it under control."

Cole took my hand, sending a shiver up my arm and right through my chest. I reached into my purse and clicked my phone on to silent. I didn't want anything interrupting this night.

I turned to point Cole in the direction of the pub, and out of the corner of my eye I caught sight of a figure hunched up in front of the crystal shop across the street. He wore dark grey jeans, and a grey hoodie, the hood pulled tight around his face. He turned away as I looked at him, but not before I'd caught a glimpse of his face.

My whole body convulsed, the reaction visceral. I would recognised that sandy blonde hair, slightly crooked nose and baby blue eyes anywhere.

It was *Ethan*.

8

BELINDA

"What's wrong?" Cole squeezed my hand.

"I ..." I looked up again. The hooded figure was gone. I blinked, suddenly not so sure. There were plenty of blonde-haired, blue-eyed guys around. The jeans and hoodie didn't look like the kind of clothing Ethan would ever wear. And besides, Ethan wouldn't be so stupid as to come back to Crookshollow, especially not to hang around outside my shop.

"Belinda, talk to me." Cole's voice was gentle. "You look as though you've seen a ghost."

"It's nothing," I shook my head, trying to ward off the awful feeling in the pit of my stomach. *It's not him. It can't be him.* Ethan would be in the Cayman Islands, or Jamaica, or some other paradise where he could fritter away his ill-gotten gains. I was obviously nervous about being around Cole, so my mind was concocting the image of Ethan as a way to deal with my fear. "I thought I saw someone I recognised, but it was just a coincidence."

Cole ran his fingers over my knuckles, making my hand buzz with energy. "We don't have to go out, you know. We can just stay here and—"

"No," I said firmly, forcing the image of the figure from my mind. "I want to go. Please, Cole. Let's not speak of this anymore. I'm just overtired. I'm freaking myself out over nothing."

At *Tir Na Nog* – an Irish pub at the end of a dark, narrow alley just around the corner from the bakery – Cole asked me what I wanted to drink. He went to the bar and had a hushed conversation with the man behind it – another tall, dark-haired, muscled and heavily tattooed guy. While they were having their discussion, I forced myself not to look around the pub for the grey-hooded man. *He's not here. It's not him. Now calm down and enjoy yourself. This is the first real date you've had since Ethan left.*

Cole came back to our table a few minutes later carrying a beer and my G&T.

"What did you do?" I asked Cole as he set down our drinks. "You didn't pay for these? He didn't ask for any money? I hope you're not intending to do a runner on our tab, because I'm not wearing the shoes for that."

"See that guy behind the bar?" Cole leaned toward me, his voice lowered. "He's another Bran. His name is Mikael, and his masters are the Carnarvons, sworn enemies of the Morchards. He owes me a favour, so he's not going to tell anyone we were here, and he's not going to charge us for our meals."

"And you can trust this guy?" I glanced back over at the bar again. Mikael scowled at customers as he poured another pint, his thick arms slamming glasses down on the bar with unnecessary force. He looked as if he could rip someone's head off without expending much effort, and also as if the thought of doing so appealed to him. "He doesn't look that trustworthy to me."

"I don't look very trustworthy, either." Cole sipped his beer. "Do you trust me?"

I took a second to think about that. Despite Cole's rough appearance, and his ridiculous overconfidence and his annoying tendency to make me blush, I *did* trust him. He had been kind to me. Even though we were from two different worlds, we both had secrets, we both had situations we wanted to escape. He had a way of smiling that made me feel as if everything in the world was going to be okay. I knew I was moving too fast, that I was putting myself at risk of getting hurt again, but I didn't care. I needed this, I needed to believe things could get better.

"Fair point," I conceded.

"It is, and don't worry. Bran aren't liars. Mikael may be an enemy of my masters, but he's not *my* enemy. I learned long ago that at the end of the day, you have to be able to trust your own kind."

"That makes sense." I leaned in closer. "So what else were you talking about with this Mikael?"

"He was giving me some news," Cole said. "Mikael's master's make him work here at the pub so he can report town gossip to them. He has a real ear to the ground for anything unusual going on. Mikael and I were actually planning to go rogue together. We've been plotting it carefully for months, but my impromptu disappearance has messed things up. I was hoping he'd found the witch he was looking for, who might've been able to rid me of *this*." He tapped his ring angrily against the table. "But no such luck. He says I have to be careful. Apparently, my disappearance has caused quite a stir locally. There aren't many rogue Bran around these days. Most of the known birds were killed in ... an accident, some months back."

I decided I wasn't quite ready to hear more about witches. "Sounds intense. What's a rogue?"

"Rogue Bran don't serve a master. They either were born of Rogue parents, or they find a way to sever the bond with their master. In rare cases, their masters grant them freedom, but that hardly ever happens. Mine certainly wouldn't."

"What happened in this accident? Did it only affect rogues?"

"A few months ago, there was quite a convergence of shapeshifters in Crookshollow, and they were all rogues or other kinless beasts: foxes that left their packs, stags that have no herd, hundreds of rogue crows and ravens. All these creatures served a powerful lone wolf, named Isengrim."

"What happened? Where is this Isengrim now?"

"Dead, as are most of the rogues. Isengrim was killed at a gallery opening, although no one knows that's what happened. You might have seen something about it in the paper, the artist claimed it was a piece of *performance* art."

"I don't remember—" I choked on my drink as something clicked in my mind. "Hang on a second, was this at the Raynard exhibition opening at the Halt Institute?"

"That's the one. Were you there?"

"No, but my friend Alex was. She's Ryan Raynard's fiance."

Cole leaned back in his chair. "That *is* interesting. She never mentioned anything to you about Isengrim being a werewolf?"

"She certainly didn't. She just said a man came uninvited to the opening, and he had some grudge against Ryan for something that happened in art school. There was a scuffle, and it very nearly interrupted the performance art piece Ryan had planned. Ryan's work is all about nature, so there was a symbolic fight between a fox and a wolf ... are you telling me that was *real?*"

"Oh yes, and before that there was a huge battle on the outskirts of the town. It all ended in a big smoking hole in the earth. It's interesting that your friend hasn't told you about it."

"I guess she never thought I'd believe her." I shrugged. I couldn't believe Alex knew about this world of shifters and magic. "I can't imagine why. Plus, Ryan spent years living as a recluse. I imagine he prefers to keep things private ..." A thought suddenly occurred to me. "Hey, are you suggesting that Ryan is some kind of shifter?"

"I'm not suggesting anything," Cole smirked, downing the rest of his beer and passing me the menu. He cracked his open and surveyed the options. "Should we order? They're going to close the kitchen at ten."

"Why is this going on here? Why in Crookshollow this hotbed of shifter activity?"

"I'm going to have the steak." Cole put down the menu. "What about you?"

"You're ignoring me."

"I'm just trying to have a date with a gorgeous woman," Cole grinned. "And all you want to talk about is your friend and her famous artist fiancé. I'm starting to worry I won't measure up."

"I thought we were supposed to be sharing all our secrets. You have to tell me about Ryan! Why was there a huge fight? What explosion?"

"This isn't my secret. It's your friend's secret, and I'm not spilling any more. The rest of it is ancient history. It has nothing to do with me or why I left the Morchards. I thought you wanted to know about me."

"I have to understand your world, which is quite new and scary. My world is very small, and since you spent the day in the bakery, you've pretty much seen all of it. I'm just trying to get a sense of it all. And I'll have the pulled pork sandwich, thanks."

"There's also a peanut butter cheesecake on the dessert menu."

I grinned. "Sold."

Cole took the menus up to the bar, ordered our food, and returned with another drink for each of us. As I sipped the G&T, the alcohol and Cole's gorgeous eyes making my head spin, he started to talk again. "Fine, if you want a history lesson, we can talk about Crookshollow. What do you know about the town's paranormal history?"

"Not a lot." I shrugged, taking another long sip of my drink. "We studied it in school, of course, but I was never that interested. Home economics and chemistry were more my subjects."

"Chemistry?"

"Sure. All baking is chemistry – mixing different things in a controlled environment to produce reactions. It's delicious science."

Cole laughed. The sound made my insides flip around again. "Delicious science. I like that. I hope we can do more delicious science together tomorrow."

He rolled his tongue over his bottom lip. I nearly dropped my glass. "D-d-definitely." I managed to stutter out.

"Good. So, if you think back to your history lessons, you probably remember that the whole of Loamshire was famous as a place where witches congregated? Crookshollow village itself sits at the crossroads of two important ley lines."

"What are those?"

"They're lines across the landscape that link important ceremonial or spiritual sites. In some cases they are simply veins of energy coursing through the earth, but here in Crookshollow, they are actual lines – straight pathways linking important sites of the worship of the old gods. Ancient peoples gathered here to worship deities of the earth and the stars and the seasons. And with them came their familiars, and the other magical races, who have lived in secret among humans since the dawning of our time." His eyes darkened, their smouldering depths holding all kinds of secrets. "My master's family came to this land with their horses and weapons and Christian god, and they made it their mission to drive out the infidels."

"You don't like them much."

"They're hypocrites, first of all. My master boasts of his ancestors being some of the most prolific witch hunters in all of Britain, and yet they have kept Bran for centuries. They don't give a fuck about religion and what it has to say about magic and witches, until it suits them. What they want is control."

"Cole … why did you run away?" I nestled my hand on top of his, and was surprised to feel it shake slightly beneath mine. "I mean, I know your master was cruel, but I gather he's been that way your whole life. What made you finally decide to just leave?"

He sighed, and retracted his hand, his fingers going to touch the black ring, then jerking away again. "I was given an order, and I don't want to obey it."

"But couldn't you just say that?" I gestured at all six foot of gloriously muscled him. "I mean, there can't be that many people in the world who could argue with you, could there?"

"A Bran is not allowed to disobey an order from his master. That powerful piece of magic was bound into our DNA. My brother thinks it was placed there by Odin himself, to prevent his ravens Hugin and Muninn from using the secrets they heard throughout Midgard to make their own fortunes." Cole must've seen me looking blank, because he added. "Odin was an ancient Viking god. He had two ravens who he sent out every morning to fly across his kingdom and bring him back all the news. But no one ever thinks about what that life must have been like for those ravens – what happened to them when they brought Odin news he did not like? How did people react when they saw the ravens and knew Odin was watching them? It is not a happy life, to be someone's servant."

"So what happens? There is no punishment from disobeying. You disobeyed and apart from your finger, you seem fine."

"Technically, I haven't outright disobeyed the order. Not yet," Cole said. "I just haven't carried it out yet. And there is definitely a punishment. "He touched the ring, and winced again.

"It's that painful?"

He nodded. "Every hour I spend away from my master, the pain grows worse. I am magically bound to the Morchard family, until they willingly release me. The ring is what enables Victor to control me, to use my power for himself. It's what forces my body to obey whatever he commands of me. I'm trying to fight it, but I'm weakening. In a couple of days I'll be crawling back toward the castle, begging for him to forgive me."

His casual tone startled me. How could he be so calm, with such a terrible burden hanging over his head. And what happened if he couldn't fight the pain? "Can you break the link?"

Cole shook his head. "Not yet, but at the moment, that's the least of my worries."

"The fact you are in agony is the least of your worries? You're nuts. What was the order, anyway?"

"Victor Morchard had sold me to another family. Apparently, he had some debts to pay off, and this new family were in need of a Bran, so an exchange was agreed. My new master – Sir Thomas Gillespie – is currently travelling to Loamshire from the North to make the exchange."

"You mean, Thomas Gillespie the politician?"

"The one and same. The politician and ancient vampire."

Vampire? My head was starting to hurt. "I can't believe this."

"Believe it. Gillespie is over four-hundred years old, drinks the blood of humans for pleasure, and he holds no life sacred. As soon as he discovers I have run from the Morchards, he will punish them, which I'm not so upset about. But then, he will come after me, and if he catches me, I will be begging them for death before the end. As much as I loathe my master's family, Sir Thomas would be much worse. His kind take pleasure in pain and death. He would force me to do evil things, abominable things."

Cole's voice dripped with hatred. He balled his hands into fists, his rage bubbling just beneath his skin. His dark eyes turned cold, their depths stormy. He hated this new master and his family, whoever they were. *But why? What have they done?*

"How do you know what he will make you do?" I asked nervously, my fingers squeezing the straw in my drink. I didn't want to upset Cole any further, but I needed to know.

"I know," Cole whispered, his eyes on fire.

"But how? Is that one of your secrets?"

"He killed my father, Belinda. He shot my father from the sky, without reason or remorse. And then he drained him of blood."

"Cole, I—"

"That's it," he hissed, cutting me off. "You know all you need to know. I don't want to talk about it any longer."

Our food arrived then, along with a folded note. I reached for it, but Cole beat me to it. He unfolded the note, frowning as he read it. I tried to lean over his shoulder to look at its contents, but Cole hid it against his chest.

"I thought we weren't going to have any secrets."

Cole stuffed the note into his pocket. "We're not. But right now, I need to figure out a few things before I tell you about them. Sometimes it is safer for you if you are kept in the dark. Secrets can get you killed. You have to trust me on that, Belinda."

You have to trust me. That was the second time he'd spoken about trust that night. I gazed into his eyes again, and the storm there was fading. He took another drink, and when he put the pint back down on the table, he was back to his old, mischievous Cole again.

"So what about you?" he said, reaching across the table and taking my hand in his. I gasped as he turned my hand over and stroked a finger over my wrist, the sensitive skin tingling beneath his touch. I remembered that he'd called this evening a date, and gulped back a mouthful of gin. "I've spoken about my life, so now I want to know why this brilliant baker is breaking down into tears at the thought of losing a little business? Why is your apartment so empty? Why can't you afford to hire anyone when you're clearly the most popular bakery in town?"

"I'm really bad with numbers?" I stared up at Cole hopefully, my pulse quickening in fear. Now that it had come to my turn, I didn't want to tell him about it, to open my mouth and admit that I was failing, that I couldn't keep my shop afloat.

But I had promised, and Cole had kept his end of the bargain. I owed him my big secret.

I picked up my glass, and downed the rest in one long gulp. Courage thus imparted, I took a deep breath, and squeezed my eyes shut. I couldn't bear to look at him, to see his face as I spilled the whole story - my quiet, silent shame. With tears forming in my eyes, I told him about falling for Ethan, about dreaming of our wedding and our future together, about coming home to that empty house and finding out he'd gone on the run with all my stuff, about the police shutting the shop, and discovering the debt.

"I'm feel as if I'm drowning. I keep kicking my feet and pulling my head above the water, but land is so far away and I'm so very tired. I keep telling myself it's only a few more years, and then the debt will be paid off and I'll be free. But—" my voice cracked. "I'm so lost. I don't know what to do. I'm so stupid for not seeing through Ethan's lies. This is what you get for being stupid."

"You're not stupid." Cole's voice was so harsh, it made me jump. My eyes flew open, the tears trapped inside spilling down my cheeks. He stared at me across the table with a deep, intense gaze. He looked livid. "This is fucking bullshit. It's ridiculous that you're being punished for that man's crimes."

I shrugged, trying to hide my tears behind nonchalance. "It's what I deserve. I took on the responsibility of the business. It's not the government's fault that I was dating a criminal."

"Don't do that." Cole leaned across the table, so his forehead touched mine. He picked up my hands and squeezed them tightly. His eyes were so intense that they unnerved me. "Nightingale, I don't want to hear you say things like that. Don't fucking blame yourself. If you take the blame, then that bastard wins."

"But I—"

"But *nothing*. You are the victim here, nothing more. You don't have to own it. You did nothing wrong, and you shouldn't have to live with the consequences of his actions. Your shop cannot become your prison."

"I—" I started to protest, to explain that I had to take responsibility for my part in it, for not seeing what Ethan really was sooner, for being so blinded by him that I hadn't paid attention. But all that came out was a choked sob.

And as soon as that sob came out, more followed. Huge, sniffling sobs that rocked my whole body. My breakdown in the shop this morning was nothing compared to this outpouring of raw emotion. My chest felt tight, crushed beneath the weight of my pain. Cole kept a hold of my hands while I rocked against the table like a fool, tears and snot running down my face.

"Belinda." Cole dropped my hands and wrapped his arms around me, pulling me into his chest. I sobbed against his broad chest, my snotty face making a mess of his beautiful new shirt. He smelled like my deodorant, and something deep and woody and comforting. Like Fauntelroy Park in the midst of spring. The warmth of his skin surrounded me, like a hot bath washing away all my cares.

It felt so good.

"I'm sorry. I'm sorry—" I cried, trying to wipe my snot off his shirt, but only succeeding in making a bigger mess.

"You have *nothing* to be sorry for. *He'll* be sorry," Cole growled, as he steadied me on my seat. "This Ethan better hope he's really good at hiding, because ravens are very good at finding things, and when I find him, I'm going to make sure his soul doesn't find the underworld for a very, *very* long time."

COLE SWITCHED to talking about lighter subjects, movies and music and books, while we ate our food. I calmed down a bit, but once I'd started crying I couldn't seem to stop. I couldn't even taste the peanut butter cheesecake. We finished quickly, and then Cole wrapped his arm around me and let me outside. Once I got into the crisp night air, I calmed down even more. I wiped my face again, and took a deep breath, my stomach no longer churning and flipping quite as badly as before. My cheeks and nose felt hot and sticky from all the tears. I was glad I couldn't see myself in a mirror – I knew my makeup would have smudged. I probably looked like a crack-addicted raccoon. "I'm a mess." I groaned.

"I was going to say you looked like a vaudeville meerkat." Cole squeezed my arm. I snorted, and held on to him tighter. "But I still think you look beautiful. I like my girls with a bit of character. Come on, it's getting late, and we have bread to bake in the morning. Let's get you home."

I relaxed into his shoulder, allowing the warmth of his body to calm me. My stomach flipped again, but this time it wasn't from sadness. I suddenly became very aware of his hand brushing against the side of my breast.

Don't be ridiculous, I told myself. *You look like a vaudeville meerkat. He's not interested in sleeping with you, not when you're such a mess. He's just being nice. And besides, you're not interested in him, either, remember? Sleeping with Cole would be a very, very bad idea. You'll only wind up getting hurt, especially since he's messed up in this whole rogue shifter thing.*

Cole's warmth radiated through my body, his hand on the small of my back burning through my jacket. *You're not interested ... not at all ...*

Cole stumbled on the curb, his injured leg momentarily collapsing. "Fuck," he gritted his teeth, as he pulled me back under his arm. "Sorry about that. I'm not quite certain who's holding up who, here."

In all the excitement, I'd completely forgotten about his leg. I hoped it hadn't got any worse. I noticed that as Cole helped me up the stairs, he stayed off the injured leg.

When we were inside the apartment, I told Cole to take off his pants.

"Well," He raised an eyebrow. "I'm not used to the lady being so forward."

I stared at my bare feet, my cheeks flaring with heat. In my already delicate state, I felt a lump burning in my throat. I was dangerously close to crying again. *Why did I keep saying this kind of thing around him?* It was like I couldn't help it, all my words got jumbled and all that came out was filthy and he clearly wasn't interested in me like that, he just loved teasing, and so I was just embarrassing myself. "I didn't mean like *that.* I just want to have a look at your leg. You've been walking on it a bit tonight."

"As you wish." Cole kicked off his pants, and stretched out along the couch, his boxers doing little to disguise the bulge between his legs. I blushed deeper as I bent over his thigh, deliberately keeping my eyes focused on the wound. "It looks a lot better, actually," I said matter-of-factly. "But it still hurts?"

"Oh yes, especially when I put weight on it. But it's getting better. I barely notice it now through the pain from the ring. The big test is if it will stop me from flying," Cole said.

"Should you find out?" I gestured to the room. "Go on, change into a bird and fly."

Cole looked serious for a moment. "Belinda, are you sure you want to see that? At the moment, all this shifter stuff is theoretical to you, but once you see me change, that's it. You'll never be able to look at the world the same way again."

"Cole, it's fine. It's more important that you get better. I can't do anything about magical bonds, but at least I can help you heal your leg."

"No." He grabbed my arm. "No, Belinda, you need to be sure. My world is not the nicest place to be at times. I've already involved you more than I ever wished to, by allowing you to bring me here, and by staying."

"That's right, I'm involved already. So just change into the damn bird." I walked across the room, and closed the door to my bathroom, locking away Chairman Meow, who was sound asleep in the sink.

"As you wish." Cole stood up and pulled off the snot-covered shirt. Now he wore only his new boxer shorts, black socks and that black ring around his finger. I saw the skin around the ring was even more red and angry than this morning. It must be excruciating. Cole stared intently at a corner of the room. Neither of us said anything. I leaned against the wall, curious to see what a shift would look like.

At first, Cole didn't seem to change at all. The thought crossed my mind that maybe he had been playing me this whole time, but it was quickly dismissed when I saw his nose grow.

It extended out from his face, growing long and thin and turning black at the end as though he'd got frostbite. His strong chin extruded also, and the two came together as his face distorted, stretching and tapering, the skin becoming hard and brittle, the nostrils elongating until he became unrecognisable.

Cole threw his deformed head back and thrust his arms out. From his chest sprouted black feathers, growing out from his skin so that it seemed as if his tattoos came to life. His arm bones cracked and snapped as they grew longer, and thin bones extended out from his skin, sinew forming between them. All along his arms, the black feathers sprouted, growing larger as they fanned out to cover his skin. As they moved over each other, they rustled like autumn leaves being blown across the ground.

As I watched transfixed by the strange display before me, Cole shrank down toward the floor. His body pulled itself inward, becoming more compact, folding in on itself like a collapsible tent. His knees bent backwards, cracking loudly as they moved back from his torso, completely altering his centre of gravity. Cole leaned forward, his beak tapping the ground, and from his arse sprouted a wedge-shaped tail. He was now completely coated in silky black feathers, and he turned up to look at me. All that was left of the Cole I knew was those piercing, intelligent eyes.

"Caw?"" The raven croaked.

"That's amazing," I breathed.

Cole nodded. He took a few steps across the floor, his injured leg supporting his weight without much effort. Behind me, Chairman Meow clawed at the door, wailing that his new bird friend was waiting to play with him.

"Everything looks good so far," I said, suddenly feeling very odd talking to a bird and knowing he understood me. I talked to Chairman Meow all the time but I knew in the back of my head he was wondering why I couldn't stop yammering so he could sleep in peace. "Can you fly?"

The raven hopped up on to the counter and launched himself over the edge. I lunged forward, certain he was going to drop straight on to the floor and injure himself further, but two enormous black wings unfurled elegantly from its body. They flapped twice, lifting Cole up toward the ceiling. He seemed a little shaky at first, but quickly found his groove. Soon he was zooming around the dim lightbulb in lopsided circles.

"Yay, Cole!" I clapped. It might have been my imagination, but the way the crow's beak was shaped, it almost appeared as if he were grinning.

"Croak!" Cole announced, and flew down the stairwell. Before I could follow him, he zoomed past again, this time heading for my bedroom. "Hey!" I called after him. "Stay out of my underwear drawer!"

All I heard in reply was a defiant squawk.

While Cole was flying around in my bedroom, I spied his jeans lying on the floor. The note Mikael had given him peeked out of the pocket. My fingers itched to grab it. After all, it had something do with Cole, which meant that it concerned me. If either one of these families were coming after him, it could place the bakery in danger.

No, I told myself. *It's Cole's business. It's up to him to tell you what's in the note. You promised him that you'd trust him, so don't break that promise a mere two hours later.*

I heard a thud. Startled, I looked up, feeling guilty for even thinking about reading the note. Behind the bathroom door, Chairman Meow howled about injustice. Cole walked out of the bedroom in his naked, human form.

"I can fly," he said, pumping his fist in the air. "And my leg feels a lot better. You know your stuff, Nightingale."

His leg *did* look a lot better. I stared at it in awe, trying hard not to allow my gaze to wander to other parts of him. It was strange, because a wound that deep and nasty shouldn't have healed up so fast. I mentioned this to Cole, and he nodded.

"Bran heal faster than typical humans," he explained. "It's got something to do with the inherent energy required to sustain our ability to shapeshift. All shapeshifting species heal incredibly quickly."

"Wow, that's a pretty cool superpower," I said, still avoiding looking at his body. "Are you immortal?"

Cole snorted. "That would be wonderful, wouldn't it? All these aristocratic families with the same Bran serving them generation after generation. They wouldn't even have to train a new butler. No, I'm not immortal, as I may well discover if I can't find some way to get this damn ring off. By the way, I may have landed on your bed. It's not very soft."

I sighed. "Tell me about it. Are you going to put some clothes on?"

"What's the matter, sweetheart? All of this making you nervous?" Cole ran his hands over his taut chest and muscular thighs. *Damn.* I bit my lip. He was so cocky, so sure of himself. And he looked so good. I wondered what that chest would feel like pressed up against my back—

I pretended to be busy making a cup of tea, so he couldn't see me blushing. "I just figured you'd be sick of walking around without them. Or at least you'd like to take a shower. You don't want to end up like me, always smelling faintly of bread."

"I like the way you smell. It reminds me of being in the kitchens at the castle before a big feast.' He yawned and stretched his arms above his head. "That shower sounds like a great idea."

"Fine, but open that door at your peril. The Chairman is ready to go postal."

"I think you'd better take care of that. If you could keep that cat in with you again, I'd appreciate it. I think he can smell raven on me."

I pulled open the door and grabbed a scrabbling Chairman Meow by the scruff of the neck. As soon as I was cradling him in my arms like a baby, he calmed down and started purring, rubbing his cheeks against my arm as I rubbed his tummy the way he liked. He shot Cole a furious glance, as if to say, "Don't you get comfortable here. This is *my* human." Cole gave the cat's tail an amused tweak, then went inside the bathroom and shut the door.

A few moments later, I heard the shower running. I fed Chairman Meow, and then dawdled in the kitchen, fixing myself a mug of tea. I tried to tell myself it wasn't so I could see Cole's body again when he came out.

He'd left all his clothes on the floor. I stared at that puddle of dark fabric, my heart hammering against my chest. I lifted the corner of his shirt and brought it to my face, and breathed in deeply. His rich, woody scent came off, making my stomach flip. I dropped the shirt again. *This is ridiculous. You're just driving yourself crazy.*

I glanced down at the jeans again. I could see the white corner of the note sticking out of the pocket. With a glance to the closed door of the bathroom, I reached down and pulled the note out. It was written on the back of an order pad. I could see the list of meals for the table next to ours scrawled across the front. I unfolded it and glanced over the other side.

The message puzzled me:

Harry Morchard is dead.

Huh? Someone died? I recognised the name Morchard. It was someone related to Cole's master. What did that mean? Did Cole have something to do with it?

I heard the shower shut off. Heart racing, I shoved the note back into Cole's pocket and tossed his jeans on the floor. I grabbed my tea from the counter and was bringing it to my lips as he cracked open the door.

He stared at me, I stared at him. An awkward moment passed between us. My heart pounded against my chest as I wondered if he was going to ask me to spend the night with him, and what I might say to that.

Cole's gaze lingered on my face, and my half-filled tea cup. "So ... goodnight, I guess." He scratched his head, and a long black ringlet flopped over his eye.

"I have to use the bathroom."

"Right," he stepped aside.

He didn't make any move to squeeze my ass as I moved past him. In fact, he didn't even meet my eyes. I went into my bedroom to grab my things, my whole mood sinking. So he wasn't interested in me after all. I mean, surely he would have made a move by now? It was the perfect time. I thought we had a chemistry, but maybe ... I was just imagining it.

Guys like Cole love to flirt. It's a game to them. I reminded myself. *You can't take everything he says at face value, or you'll end up with a broken heart again. He's just not into you, and that's probably for the best.*

I knew the annoying voice in my head was right, but I still felt bitter and disappointed. I finished my teeth and turned out the light. Cole had already settled himself on the couch with a blanket, Chairman Meow curled contentedly at his feet.

"Traitor," I glowered at the Chairman. He opened one lazy eye and winked at me.

"Goodnight, Nightingale," Cole said, flashing me one of those killer smiles. But this time, it didn't flip my stomach the way it usually did. Because I knew he didn't really mean it. He was just being nice, the only way he knew how.

I picked up Chairman Meow, and moved toward my bedroom, my good mood from earlier deflating like a balloon. "Yeah, goodnight."

9

COLE

I waited an hour, occasionally getting up and pressing my ear against Belinda's door. Finally, I heard her deep, regular breathing. She was asleep.

She'd given me such a hurt look after I said goodnight to her. Clearly, she wanted me. All her blushing and turning away and covering her face with her hair made that pretty obvious. I wanted to say something, to let her know that I wanted her just as badly. I knew she was waiting for me to make the first move, and I was ready to tear all her clothes off.

But I was desperately trying to delay that move as long as possible. Hopefully so long it would never happen.

I'd made myself a promise, and damnit, I would keep it, even if it killed me. I wasn't going to get involved with anyone emotionally while I was still a slave.

I'm no good for you. I stared at Belinda's shut door, willing the message to somehow enter her head so she wouldn't have to look at me as though I'd just told her Christmas was cancelled. *You'll figure that out pretty damn soon, and you'll be glad we didn't fuck.*

Getting that note from Mikael had really freaked me out, and that had made me more cautious around Belinda than I might otherwise have been, especially with her wearing that slinky black dress. Unusually for me, my mind was too preoccupied for sex.

Almost too preoccupied. That dress hugged her tiny body in *all* the right places.

No. I had to focus. I needed to see for myself how Harry Morchard's death had come to be. Mikael didn't know, or he would have told me. I was supposed to be watching Harry, which meant that Victor would blame me for his death. And if it was in any way connected to my disappearance ... I was in deep, deep trouble.

I needed to do what ravens did best – watch and listen and find out what I could.

The last thing I wanted to do was leave Belinda alone. But I didn't know what else to do. As long as the Morchards still believed I was dead, I was perfectly safe. I hoped.

Belinda's door creaked inward. I stepped back, heart pounding. *Just tell her you were getting a drink of water. Thank fuck you didn't start shifting already.*

But it was only Chairman Meow, pushing the door open with his nose. He saw me staring down at him and gave me a pleading look.

"Meow?"

"I'm not feeding you," I whispered to the cat, waving my arms in a gesture that clearly implied I wanted him to go away. Of course, being a cat, this just made him climb up my leg and wail louder.

"Meow! Meeeeeow!"

"Under any other circumstances, you'd be trying to eat me," I laughed, giving the little dude a scratch behind the ears. "Look after her for me."

Against Chairman Meow's protests, I went into the bathroom and closed the door.

I'd observed as I was flying around earlier that there were only three windows in Belinda's flat, a tiny one overlooking the alley behind the shop, and two larger ones looking over the high street below. One was in her bedroom, and I wasn't going in there. The other was here in the bathroom. I pulled the sash up, and a gust of crisp air blew in, knocking a bottle of hand cream off the edge of the sink, where it clattered loudly against the chipped enamel. I cringed at the noise and stood still, listening. But I didn't hear Belinda stir, and her light stayed off.

I pushed the sash right the way open. Then, taking a deep breath, I forced a change.

Changing your shape is such a strange experience. You are you still, but everything *feels* different. Your nose is still attached to your face, but it's no longer your nose. You still control your legs, but now they bend a completely different way. For the first ten minutes after you change, everything feels completely alien, you can't remember which way your neck is supposed to turn. Even though I'd changed thousands of times in my life, I never got used to the sensation.

I grabbed the edge of the sink and gritted my teeth as my face shifted first, my skin stretching and becoming the long, hard beak. The feathers burst from my skin – they itched badly, and I longed to scratch the crawling sensation that covered my body. But I kept my hands against the sink, because the worst was coming.

My bones cracked and mutated, the sinews reconfiguring into new shapes. It freaked me out too much if I thought about it, so I tried to stare straight ahead and wait until it was over. My eyes wobbled and my vision blurred as the irises changed, becoming the predatory vision of the raven. I blinked, and suddenly, the bathroom appeared completely different.

My eyes have ciliary muscles that can change the shape of my lens rapidly. Ravens also see in four colour spectrums, so now the previously drab bathroom came alive with brilliant ultraviolet colours. I flapped my wings, testing the strength and stability of my leg. It was one thing to fly around Belinda's tiny flat, but quite another to soar over the countryside without being spotted.

Everything seemed fine. Time to move out.

I hopped up on the windowsill, unfurled my wings, and took off. The warm air rising from the streets below created the current on which I soared. I swooped down, my eyes searching around me for any sign that I was being followed. So far, so good.

Below me, the streets were mostly empty. Houses glowed with lights from bedrooms and televisions. A lone pizza delivery van weaved down the narrow streets. A couple of drunk guys wandered out from the pub, holding each other around the shoulders and singing 'Bohemian Rhapsody' at the top of their lungs.

I flew over the edge of the village, across the forest where I was less likely to be spotted. I headed along the edge of the trees, toward Morchard Castle. I could already see the dark shadow of it looming on the horizon, the four imposing turrets jutting toward the heavens. As I drew closer, the ring around my wing throbbed with impatience, pulling me toward my master.

I'd sworn that I'd never go back there, and it was barely 48 hours later, and here I was again. But I had to see. I had to *know*.

The northern edge of Morchard's estate bordered up against the Crookshollow forest. I figured if I stuck to that area, I should be safe from detection. Byron usually patrolled that stretch of the border, and if my hunch was right and he had lied to Pax about hearing me fall in the water, then he was at least protecting me.

I swooped lower as I neared the castle, hoping to hide my shape below the raised garden beds. I saw lights on toward the back of the western wing, where the family lived. *Odd,* usually Victor would be in the aviary or laboratory at this time of night, while Susan would be drinking in the drawing room. I moved around the edge of the house, flying between the garden beds, then hopping along the grass, trying to stay hidden from anyone who might be looking from the house. A cold breeze blew through my feathers. I could sense another raven's presence, feel its eyes on me. Hopefully it was Byron. I guessed it was likely, since no one had attacked me yet.

At least I have one ally in this cursed place. It's odd, I never would have predicted Byron would be an ally.

The ring surged with energy, tugging me toward the back patio, calling me to my master. I peered at the scene in the garden. A table had been set out on the back patio, beside the swimming pool. The servants bustled about, setting out platters of food and filling drinks. The family were gathered around, talking in low voices to each other, heads bowed. Every one of them wore black. Behind them, stretching out from one end of the house and covering nearly half of the expansive lawn, I could see the frame of the aviary, dark now, with no one inside. I heard no screeches or chirps from within the structure – all the specimens were probably asleep. Just seeing the dark outline of the trees and structures behind the aviary's glass walls made my blood boil with rage. But I wasn't there to spy on Victor's experiments. I needed to find out what was going on.

I thought about moving closer to try and hear what they were saying (my hearing wasn't as good as my sight), but then they started to move through the garden. I hopped around to the other side of the garden bed, and watched as the family drew closer, walking in a line across the lawn. Victor and his brothers carried a long, dark box, covered with a white floral arrangement. *A coffin.* They'd got his body back from the morgue awfully quick. Susan and Victor's daughter Virginia carried tall silver candlesticks, the flickering light of the flames casting strange shadows along the paved path. Some of the extended family and three of Harry's obnoxious Eton friends trailed at the rear.

I followed at a safe distance (or as safe as I could get in this place) as the procession moved slowly along the path toward the forest, heading to the small family graveyard at the back of the private garden. A tall mausoleum dominated the space, the classical facade making it look more like a shrine to a Greek woodland goddess than a house of the dead. The heavy wrought-iron gates were propped open.

They reached the mausoleum and fanned out into a lopsided half-circle. The men lowered the casket onto a stone plinth in the centre of the mausoleum's single room, then stepped back from it as though it might bite them. I hopped over to the hedge on the edge of the path, heart pounding as I peered through the leaves. *Please don't let Pax or Poe see me ...*

Victor stood rigid in front of the family, his sandy-hair almost glowing in the moonlight. In that deep, booming voice of his, he spoke about his son, all his ambitions, all his achievements. At one point, his strong voice cracked, and he had to stop a moment to compose himself. I'd known it was true as soon as I'd seen Mikael's note, of course. Mikael had no reason to lie to me. But now, seeing them all here, their usually cruel faces wracked with grief, the reality of what this meant became terrifyingly clear.

I only heard snatches of Victor's speech, but his last words came through loud and clear, his voice dripping with vengeance. "... my son, who was brutally set upon by vampire thugs just as he got off the train ... his blood drained ... taken in the prime of his life ... Those who are responsible for my son's murder will pay for what they've done."

My blood turned cold. The ring tightened so hard, I struggled for breath. He was talking about me.

Victor stepped aside and put his arms around the shoulders of his ice-queen of a wife. They both bowed their heads as Victor's younger brothers pushed Harry's coffin into its niche in the mausoleum. Virginia blew out the candles. They shut and locked the doors, and returned to the patio, where the servants waited with champagne, whisky and all kinds of illicit drugs to help the family drown their pain.

So it was true. Harry Morchard was dead, and he'd been killed by a vampire. That could only mean one thing: Thomas Gillespie knew I was gone, and he's sending a message to the Morchards. *Bring me my property, or else.*

I was dead meat.

10

BELINDA

I woke up to something poking my eye.

"Meow!"

It was Chairman Meow. He shoved his paw into my eye socket again, a favourite trick of his to get my attention. Obviously there was some urgent matter to attend to. "Go away," I mumbled, pulling the covers up around my chin. I was so tired. I just wanted to sleep some more. Light peeked in from the bedroom window, casting a faint glow across the Chairman's concerned face.

Light ... the sun was coming up. But that didn't make sense. I got up well before the sun came up ...

It was then I became dimly aware of the buzzing sound behind me.

I picked up my phone from where it was vibrating across the windowsill. I stared groggily at the time, not understanding. How could it be so late? My alarm hadn't even gone ...

Shit.

I'd forgotten to turn my phone off silent from last night. I'd slept through my alarm. It was 5:26AM. I was late.

"Double shit!"

I leapt out of bed, catapulting Chairman Meow into the pile

of laundry I'd stacked in the corner for when I could afford to go to the laundromat (yes, Ethan took the washing machine). I groped around, still half asleep, for something appropriate to wear. I scrambled through the shoebox that currently held my clean underwear, found an old pair of panties, but no bra. *Fuck.* I tugged on some socks. *No time for a bra.* I pulled on a wrinkled shirt and a pair of black jeans, jammed my hair up into a bun, and raced into the living room.

Cole wasn't on the couch or in the bathroom. I didn't have time to worry about him, though. I cracked open a tin of cat food and threw it on the floor, where Chairman Meow pounced on it eagerly. I raced downstairs, my mind frantically going over all my options. *The bread will be an hour late, but maybe I could run over to The Happy Baker and grab some of their loaves to tide me over. I'll have to skip the cakes today, and—*

I stopped short, my chest heaving. Cole was standing in the kitchen, hairnet firmly in place, and faded black apron tied around his waist. He'd plugged in my iPod, and was humming to himself as he shuffled around to my 80s playlist, pulling tray after tray of freshly baked bread and pies from the oven.

Holy shit. He's done the work. He's done all *the work.*

"So," I folded my arms, trying to keep my hands from shaking. "You're hooked on a feeling, are you?"

Cole whirled around, and gave me one of his patented killer grins. "Good morning, sleepyhead."

I peered over his shoulder at the rows of neatly-formed loaves rising in their pans. Tears formed at the corners of my eyes, and I rubbed my face, trying to pretend it was just sleep and not a surge of emotion I was trying to stave off. "I can't believe you did this all by yourself. Why didn't you come and get me?"

"I did, when I heard your phone buzzing, but you muttered something impolite, rolled over, and went back to sleep again."

"I don't remember that."

"I'm sorry. I know I should have woken you. You just looked so peaceful, as though you hadn't slept properly in months, so I decided to let you rest. Don't worry," he gestured to the fully-intact kitchen. "I haven't burned anything yet, *and* I've kept most of the flour inside the bread this time."

"How could you hear my alarm going off? It was on silent, that's how come I didn't hear it."

"Bran have great hearing." Cole finished off another loaf and placed it in the pan. "20/20 vision, too. That's how I could see that even in the dark, you drool when you sleep. It's adorable. Hey, are you not wearing a bra?"

I turned away, furiously wiping away the tears in my eyes. "Thank you," I whispered, dangerously close to choking up. *You have to get it together. This isn't a big deal. So he did something nice for you. He's a nice guy, underneath all that danger and cockiness. It doesn't mean anything.*

It can't mean anything.

"No problem. Now stop blubbering, throw on one of those ugly hairnets, and come help me. And don't you dare go upstairs to change your clothes. You're going to have to take care of the cakes. I tried to ice one but it ended up looking like some strange modern art piece."

I couldn't believe how many people showed up at the bakery. When I threw the doors open at 6AM, there was already a small group waiting outside. Word about Finn's dismissal must have spread like wildfire through the village.

Or, perhaps the bakery's newfound popularity had nothing to do with the fact Finn was no longer behind the counter. Perhaps it had more to do with a certain sexy raven who was serving up coffee and cakes with a cheeky grin. Not only were the Knit n' Bitch club in for an "impromptu brunch meeting," but the Crookshollow Floral Society decided to hold their AGM at the table in front of the sweets cabinet, and the local Historical Walking Group popped in for a post-workout treat. The bakery looked like it was the set from an episode of *Last of the Summer Wine*.

I left Cole to deal to his adoring fans, and kept myself busy behind the counter refilling the displays, answering the phone (which was ringing off-the-hook with cake orders) and whipping up five batches of cookies. I could see just by the scone demand that we were probably going to sell out early today, too.

I pulled another tray of melting moments out of the oven and set them out on the cooking racks. I took down the cake stand that had once held a batch of lemon scones, (but now held only a few crumbs,) and cleaned that before loading it up again. I was busy repositioning the stand on the counter, when a deep voice broke through my thoughts.

"Hey, gorgeous."

I looked up, startled, and stared into the eyes of a dark-haired, leather-clad biker. His strong jaw and deep brown eyes reminded me of Cole, but he was older, his dark eyes crinkling at the corners. Even though his smile was casual, his whole body seemed tense, a snake coiled before the strike. The way he kept his eyes glued to mine gave me an uneasy feeling, and his presence smacked of *déjà vu*. It was only two days ago that I was standing in the same spot and staring gape-mouthed at Cole.

"Can I help you?" I asked, trying to keep myself poised.

"I heard you have a new assistant in here," the biker said. "I'd like to speak to him."

Cole? My body froze. The old biddies asking about my sexy new counter boy were one thing, but if this guy was asking for Cole by name ... it had to be connected to Cole's escape from his master.

"Um, I—" I flicked my eyes over to where Cole was standing. He was in the middle of packaging up a small cheesecake for a grinning single mum, but his eyes kept flicking over toward me and the tall biker. Cole finished the transaction, then sauntered over to us, his eyes blazing.

"Go away." Cole hissed across the counter, as he filled a bag of melting moments for a customer.

The biker shook his head. "I have to talk to you."

"You can't *be* here. They will be following you, especially after what happened. You'll lead them right to me."

"So you heard about Harry? Shocking stuff. Don't worry, I was careful. Come on," the man shrugged his shoulder towards the back of the shop.

"Come on where?"

"There must be a kitchen or storage cupboard back there? We need to talk."

"I'm not going anywhere with you," Cole glowered. "And if you keep harassing me, Belinda is going to pound your ass with her awesome karate skills. Now, if you'll excuse me, I have croissants to put out."

"Cole, you're being ridiculous—"

"We're done here." Cole turned away from the biker and started cleaning the counter with rough, furious strokes. The biker stared at him for a few minutes, opening his mouth as if he wanted to say more. But then he shrugged, as if the entire exchange meant nothing to him, and walked out, slamming the door shut behind him so hard the frame rattled.

"Who was that?" I asked, leaning against the counter while I waited for my heart rate to return to normal.

"Nobody important," Cole barked, in a tone that clearly implied the opposite. He started to toss fresh croissants into a wicker basket with all the enthusiasm of a Chelsea football player.

"That's bullshit, and you know it. He was a Bran, wasn't he? Does this mean your master knows where you are?" Cole didn't look up. He kept slamming croissants into the basket. "Cole, look at me. This is important. Is the bakery in danger?"

Cole's back stiffened. He set down the basket and turned to look at me, his eyes flicking over my face as if he was seeing me for the first time.

"You're right, Belinda," Cole said, his eyes flashing. "I need you to be calm. But it's entirely possible we're not safe here any longer."

"We?"

"If they've seen me here, than they've seen you, too. And that means you could be a target. Victor Morchard is just the kind of man to try to get to me through you." He balled his hands into fists and kicked the counter so hard the coffee machine rattled. "Fuck!"

I cringed. Two woman waiting for their coffees gasped and bent their heads to whisper to each other. I grabbed Cole by the arm and dragged him into the kitchen, in case he scared any more customers.

"Cole, it's okay. We'll figure something out—"

"This is all my fault." he moaned. "I shouldn't have stayed here. I put you in danger. This is so much worse than I feared."

"Hey, you warned me, and I asked you to stay. I knew what I was getting into."

"No, Belinda. You don't. You really don't."

"Well, okay." I placed a hand tentatively on his shoulder. "Maybe I don't, but you do. So we're not safe anymore. We need to go somewhere we *are* safe. You need to come up with a plan. So, what's the plan, Cole? What are you going to do?"

Cole remained silent for a few moments, and then the corner of his lip curled up into a grin. "I think you might have given me the answer. We're going out tonight. But this time, it's all business. Do you have your friend Alex's number?"

I nodded.

"Call her and ask her if we can visit that fiancé of hers tonight. Tell her you met someone who desperately needs to talk to him. I don't suppose you have a car?"

I shook my head. "What do you think Ethan used to haul all my stuff away with? But don't worry, we can get Alex and Ryan to come here and pick us up. They'll be happy—"

Cole shook his head. "No, it's too dangerous. I don't want them getting caught up in anything, too. We'll go to them. Don't worry, we'll take my bike."

"But you don't have your bike."

"No, but I know where it is."

WE SOLD out of food by 3:30PM, a record for me. On any other day, I'd be elated, but ever since that other biker had shown up, I couldn't focus on my work. It was all too scary. If Cole's master had found him here, what would he do? Who was that man who came into the bakery? Was that Victor Morchard? Why did he look so much like Cole? Why was he trying to get Cole to go away and talk to him – surely, if he was as angry as Cole implied, he just would have killed him on sight? Cole didn't look as though he were afraid of the biker, just angry with him.

I tried to question Cole about it, but he brushed me off. "It will take a long time to explain," he said, as he took dripping dishes out of the sink and placed them in the rack to dry. "I'll answer all your questions tonight. In the meantime, let's just focus on getting the work done."

Alex had returned my text at lunchtime and said she and Ryan would be happy to see us for supper that evening. "Is everything okay?" she messaged. "Who's this guy?"

"You'll meet him tonight. He's wonderful. I don't think he's another Ethan. But maybe you can help me judge?"

I could barely focus on the baking, but eventually we managed to get all the slices made and the cakes decorated for the next day. We barely talked, except when Cole had questions about the recipes. He seemed twitchy, nervous. He looked up at the door every few seconds, his face puckered with concern. Chairman Meow came loping down the stairs, and Cole leapt so high into the air he practically hung from the rafters.

After we washed the last of the dishes, Cole told me to go upstairs and change into something comfortable. I found a pair of black jeans and a red shirt that didn't smell too badly of flour, and went back downstairs to meet him just as he was wiping down the last of the kitchen.

I locked up just as a car pulled up out front. It was a tiny Fiat, and I could see the faint outline of a man sitting in the front seat. My stomach flip-flopped. Should I be nervous? Am I in danger? I locked up the shop and walked apprehensively toward the vehicle. Cole held open the door for me. "This is us," he said. "Hurry up, get inside."

Nervously, I slid into the backseat. The driver turned around and gave me the thumbs up. To my surprise, I recognised Mikael from the pub. Around his index finger was a black ring, identical to Cole's.

"Are you going rogue, too?" I asked him, but he didn't reply.

Cole climbed into the passenger seat and gave Mikael some directions. Mikael nodded, and gunned the engine. We tore away from the bakery and down the high street. Soon we were speeding through the quiet streets of terraced houses, heading toward the edge of the village.

"We weren't followed?" Mikael said, in his flat Scandinavian voice.

"I don't think so," Cole replied. I peered out the back window, but couldn't see any cars or bikes behind us that followed the same route.

"You don't sound so sure?"

"No, I'm sure."

"Fine." Silence ensued. I stared down at my hands, nervously knitting and unknitting my fingers, a hundred unanswered questions tugging at my lips. We drove further and further out of the village, and turned off on to a dark country lane. I didn't recognise the area at all. Cole fired instructions at Mikael – "left here, right here." – and we kept driving, further and further from the village, until there were no houses at all, just rolling fields and in the distance, the looming darkness of the forest.

Mikael pulled over just at the edge of the forest, in an area that was designated as a public right of way, but the overgrown hedgerows and rubbish collecting at the edges suggested it was clearly seldom used. I got out of the car and leaned against the door, wondering what would happen next. Cole hiked through the bushes for a few minutes, leaving me to stand in silence next to Mikael. Cole returned dragging a large motorbike.

"Thank you," he shook Mikael's hand. "Any luck with the other thing?"

"The witch is still not answering her phone, and when I knocked on her door there was no reply. The house looks derelict, as though it's been vacant for years, but that's not necessarily an indicator of anything. I've left a message with the woman, Clara, who runs the witchcraft store, *Astarte*. She knows every witch in Loamshire. She will make contact for you and leave a message at the witch's cemetery if a suitable witch can be reached."

"Thank you, Mikael. All debts have now been paid." Cole tapped his ring. "I'll come back for you if I can figure out how to break this thing."

Mikael nodded, turned, and slid back into his car. Without another word, Mikael drove off into the gloom, leaving us completely alone on the edge of that great, dense forest.

"Scandinavians," Cole grinned. "You've gotta love them."

Cole bent down and started to fiddle with the bike. I crossed my hands over my chest, wishing I'd thought to bring a jacket. I hadn't realised we'd be going so far out of the village. Out here amongst the trees, the wind was biting cold. I checked my phone screen. It was close to 7:30PM. "We're going to be late for supper," I told Cole.

"Only a little longer, Nightingale."

The trees rustled behind us. I spun around, searching the darkness for any sign of movement. *It's just an animal, a deer or a rabbit or ...*

Cole grabbed my arm. "Get behind me," he hissed. Numb with cold and terror, I stepped behind him, struggling to see into the blackness. Getting a brainwave, I pulled my phone out again and turned the screen on, shining the light at the trees in front of us.

"Turn that off!" Cole hissed.

Before I could comply, a shadowy figure stepped out of the shadows. His deep voice cut through the still night like a knife. "Hi Cole," he said, then turned to me. "Hello, Cole's latest conquest."

The shadow stepped into the light, and I recognised him instantly. It was the biker who had come into the shop earlier today, the one Cole had been angry at and refused to talk to. In the light of my phone he looked even more like Cole, with a strand of black hair flopping over one eye. He wore a black t-shirt that revealed muscled shoulders and arms covered in tattoos.

"Byron." Cole pushed me further behind him, as if he were trying to hide my presence with his bulk. "You shouldn't be here. Why are you following me?"

"You didn't think I'd just abandon you." Byron kicked the edge of the bike's tyre with his boot. "It's because of me that you're still alive."

"It is not."

"I saw you hiding under that tree, but I told Pax I thought you'd fallen in the water. If it weren't for me they would have torn you to pieces."

"Fine," Cole gritted his teeth. "Thanks for lying for me. I know it couldn't have been easy, since you find lying so difficult."

Sarcasm dripped from his voice. "There. We're even. You can leave us alone now."

"Don't be stupid, Cole. I've come to help you. Why can't you listen to me?"

"Because your help is going to get us both killed!" Cole shouted. He must have realised that was a bad idea, for when he spoke again, he'd lowered his voice. "This is what you do. You swoop in here like you're Odin's gift to the world and start trying to run the show. Well, I'm not part of the roost anymore, I don't have to step in line. The sooner you accept that, the sooner I'll be civil."

"And the sooner *you* accept that you've made a huge mistake, we can figure out how to save your ass from your own stupidity. You're not a rogue yet, and until you are, you're my responsibility. If I managed to track you back to that bakery, it won't be long before the Morchards or Gillespies do the same thing. You're such an idiot, Cole. You should be miles away by now. You've put this girl in danger by hanging around, by introducing her to our world."

"That *girl* saved my life," Cole snarled back. "And like it or not, she's involved now. I need to stay near her, to protect her."

"How are you going to protect anyone? You must be incredibly weak by now, from the bond. I know you were there last night. You saw what Gillespie did to poor Harry, just because he'd discovered you had gone missing. Either Morchard finds you, and you're dead, or Gillespie finds you and then you going to *wish* you were dead."

As Byron talked, I watched Cole's face. *What did Byron mean by 'you were there last night'? Cole was asleep on my couch last night. He wasn't anywhere near the Morchard castle. Is this Byron mistaken? And who is this Harry? That was the name on the note. Cole knows Harry is dead because of the note, but then—*

"I have a plan," Cole said, yanking the bike upright and

swinging one leg over. Even in the gloom, I could see his face burned with rage.

"And that plan involves you riding out of here on that shitty thing with the girl on the back, yes?" Byron laughed. "You're so utterly predictable. I knew you wouldn't be able to last long without your bike, so I came here to wait for you. But it could have just as easily been Pax and Poe waiting here for you, or someone much, much worse. For the world's most intelligent bird, you're not very bright."

"I have it all under control, Byron. If you can keep your mouth and your mind shut, we will be fine. Go back to the castle and pretend everything is normal. You're good at that."

"You're never going to forgive me for what happened, are you?" Byron tipped his head to the side. "Seriously Cole, this fixation you have with your mother is unhealthy. Maybe you should see a psychiatrist."

"And you should talk to a suicide helpline, since apparently you have a death wish." Cole gunned the engine. He yelled over the roar. "Don't you ever mention her in my presence again."

What happened to Cole's mother? I stared from Cole to Byron and back again, trying to make some sense of their rapid-fire argument.

I glanced at Cole. I was starting to feel pretty angry myself. There were so many details here that I didn't know, that Cole hadn't bothered to fill in. And – as this Byron so eloquently said – I was the one whose life was in danger. Why did Cole feel I didn't need to know these things?

"Cole, I think we need to talk—" I started to say, but Cole held up his hand to silence me. *That* pissed me off. I snapped my mouth shut, biting back the urge to say something.

Byron stepped forward, crossing his arms over his broad chest. "He's coming after you next, Cole. Even if Victor has given you up for dead, Sir Thomas is nearby, and he's going to make damn sure you don't escape. And now you've got *her* involved,"

Byron indicated me with a short dip of his head. "What's the great scheme to get yourself out of this mess? Or have you jumped first and are planning to figure it out later, like always."

"Go away, Byron. This doesn't concern you."

"It very much concerns me. If Gillespie comes to me, I won't have any choice but to share what I know. And that's my own life forfeit. Besides, we're family. I'm responsible for you—"

"You're brothers?" I asked, suddenly understanding. Of course, it made perfect sense. That's why they looked so similar, and that's why Cole was so resistant of Byron's offers of help, which – despite his threatening demeanour – sounded quite sensible.

"Of course," Byron reached down and grabbed the handle-bars of Cole's bike. His eyes flicked across my face, and he laughed. "Didn't Cole tell you? Is that another secret my little brother is kept from someone he cares about? He should know by now that secrets get you into trouble."

"Get away from my bike, Byron." Cole snapped. "We're leaving. I've had enough of this."

"It's all yours," Byron dropped his hand and stepped aside, still smiling.

"Don't follow us tonight," Cole growled. "I won't have anyone else implicated. I'll get a message to you when I have a plan in place."

I looked at Cole in confusion. He looked murderous. Byron, on the other hand, wore a cat-ate-the-canary grin that was even more disturbing. What he had said sounded so reasonable, but if Cole didn't like his brother ... there must be something to that. Byron was acting threatening, and he had known to find us out here, he'd known where Cole's bike was hidden ... I tugged on Cole's hand. "He's tampered with the bike," I whispered.

"No, I haven't, although that's actually a pretty good idea." Byron grinned. "At least your girl is clever, Cole. Don't let Sir

Thomas get his hands on her. He loves clever girls, loves devouring them."

Cole growled, deep in his throat. He grabbed the handlebars of the bike and yanked it around, so it was facing away from Byron.

"I don't think we should get on that bike," I said, my heart pounding. I didn't like the way Byron was grinning at us.

"Don't worry. Byron isn't going to hurt me. He's all talk and no action." Cole tossed me a helmet. "Put that on," he said.

"Cole, I—"

"Trust me."

Trust me. I gulped. If only he knew how hard that was for me, how much he was actually asking. The truth was, I was trying to trust him, I wanted to trust him so badly. But I knew he was lying to me, he was keeping things from me, and so I couldn't trust what he said now. And worse, I didn't trust myself.

I thought I had pretty good intuition, that I could read people, that my gut would give me a sense of what's right and wrong. Well, my gut had told me Ethan was a good guy, and I'd nearly lost everything. Even though Cole's eyes looked earnest, and the way he touched me lit my body on fire, I couldn't trust myself with him completely. I wasn't strong enough.

But, the alternative was hanging around in the dark with Byron, and I wasn't particularly keen on that, either. As much as I didn't want to let Cole into my heart, I also trusted him more than the cold cruelness in Byron's eyes.

I pulled the helmet over my head, tucking my hair into the back of my shirt. I put my arms around his warm body, pressing my chest hard against his back. *Intimate.* My body surged with energy, an almost primal manifestation of my attraction to Cole, but I was too scared and angry and confused to want to act upon my desires.

"Where's your helmet?" I asked Cole. My voice came out muffled.

"I don't need one," he called back.

With a roar of the engine, we sped off. The wind whipped around me. Cole tore down the dark road, leaving the shadow of Byron far behind us. He turned a corner and the whole bike lurched to the left, the ground tilting up toward us. I squeezed my eyes shut. *We were going to tip.* I screamed inside my head, too frightened even to push sound from my mouth. *I never should have got on this bike. I never—*

The bike swung upright again, the centre of gravity shifting back to below my ass. I relaxed slightly. We swung around another corner and my body dipped. The road came up to meet me, and I had visions of myself lying on the table at the morgue with the coroner saying, "I've never had a corpse that smelled like bread before."

I'd never been on something so loud and terrifying and exhilarating. The world faded into a blurry tunnel, a wormhole in space that seemed to be sucking me in. My heart pounded against my chest, my whole body rigid with fear as I clung to Cole with every atom of energy I possessed. But, when he finally cut the engine, and the wind and the cold and the blurry tunnel died away, my body coursed with fire. The adrenaline had finally kicked in.

"How was that?" Cole grinned at me, as he kicked down the stand.

"I hated it," I said, but I couldn't stop smiling.

"I can see that." He grinned wider, wiping a strand of hair from my face. His touch seared my cheek. Dammit, why did he have to be so attractive? I needed to get answers, but all I wanted to do was throw myself at him.

I looked away from him, desperate to break the spell he had over me. I realised we were still in the middle of nowhere. Cole had parked in a small verge alongside another dark, country road. Ahead of us was a tall iron fence, many of the rungs bent or broken. An iron gate hung open, creaking gently on its hinges as it swayed in the crisp breeze. The place gave me the creeps. "Where are we?" I asked. "I thought we were going to Alex and Ryan's?"

"We are, I just need to stop here first. Have you never been here before?" I shook my head. Cole looked puzzled. "How long have you lived in Crookshollow? This place is famous. I thought everyone had been here."

"I've lived in the village for seven years," I said. "But I've never really been one for nature walks. I much prefer the pub."

Cole laughed. "This is the Witches Cemetery. Back in the 17th and 18th centuries, Crookshollow was a centre of occult worship, until the church caught wind of all the goings on and decided to make an example of the place. Some 200 witches were burned or hanged right in the village square, and the remains of many were buried here, on unconsecrated ground, far from the god-fearing gravesites."

"Oh." I glanced around at all the crooked stones. Upon closer inspection, the place was even creepier than I first thought. The entire cemetery was black, the hedges that surrounded it devoid of all leaves – even though it was spring – and the earth puckered and scorched. Many of the stones leaned out at impossible angles, or were broken in pieces. "Why is everything blackened?"

"That's a recent development. You should ask your friend Alex about it." Cole stooped low as he walked through the rows of bent tombstones. He almost appeared as if he was looking for something.

"Alex? I don't understand."

Cole grinned. "Let's just say that she and her partner Ryan—"

"—*fiancé.*"

"—right, *fiancé* Ryan were involved in a little altercation right here, a few months back. Some of my kind were involved, not just ravens, but several vulpines – fox shifters – and other shifter species as well. The resulting fire did all the damage you can see."

"There was a *fire*? How is Alex involved in all this? Is this why we're going to see her tonight?"

"I don't want to say anything more. She will tell you. But suffice it to say that you can trust Alex with my secret."

"I wish you'd trust me with your secrets."

"I do," Cole said. He took my hand and led me along another row of stones, his eyes sweeping the ground around him.

"No, Cole. You don't. You didn't tell me about Byron being your brother when he came to the diner today. You said you'd explain tonight, but you still haven't." I pulled my hand from him. "You haven't told me what Byron meant when he said he saw you last night, or who Harry is, or anything about this vampire I'm supposed to fear so much. And you haven't explained what we're doing at this cemetery. I don't think you understand that I am scared. I need to know what's *really* going on."

Cole stopped and turned toward me. He took my hands and gripped them tightly, his touch sending shivers along my arms. His dark eyes bore into mine, searching my soul for something. "I'm trying to protect you, Belinda. The less you know, the less dangerous you are to them. I don't want Morchard or Gillespie to ever see you as a threat, or your life will be over. And I couldn't stand that."

"You say that, but it doesn't feel like that's what you're doing." My voice grew higher. I gulped back a lump rising in my throat. I was dangerously close to crying. "It feels as though you're not allowing me to make my own choices about my survival. You're taking that away from me, and after everything I told you, after everything you know about me, you must be able to see that I can't deal with that."

Cole didn't say anything. His eyes shifted, their edges softening. I continued. "I know that I mean nothing to you, but I care about you, Cole. I don't want you to die. I want to help, but I can't if you keep shutting me out."

As soon as I'd said that, I wished I could take it back. I'd said too much, revealed how I was really feeling. Now he knew I liked him; I'd given him that power over me. I stepped back, trying to tug my hands free of his, but he squeezed them tighter.

Cole's eyes flickered. I poised myself for his rejection.

"How can you say that?" Cole whispered, his voice pained. "How can you say you mean nothing to me? You saved my life."

"I'm just some girl in a bakery," I said, my voice catching. "Who doesn't even know karate. As Byron said, I'm only the next in a long line of women who are falling ... who have been in your life. I'm not the first, or the last. I'm expendable. I know that, I just—"

"I'll show you how fucking expendable you are."

Cole's lips met mine with such tremendous force I nearly fell backwards. He steadied me with one hand in the small of my back, and the other against my neck, drawing my head up toward him. Fire raced through my body as his lips parted mine, and his tongue wrapped around mine, furiously devouring me.

I rose up to meet him, shocked by the force behind his kiss. My hands reached up and tangled in his long hair, the silky strands falling through my fingers. A strand fell over my face, tickling the skin of my cheek. My whole body felt as if it were made of electricity, a great shining ball of light. Everywhere he touched hummed with energy.

Cole kissed with a need so powerful, it squeezed at my chest. His fingers splayed across the small of my back, drawing my body against him. His hardness rubbed against my thigh, and the thought of it there made me ache. It had been so long, and he was so gorgeous, and his kisses made me feel like I was sinking into a puddle of ecstasy.

My tongue slid over his, the heat of his mouth pulling me in, drawing out all my doubts, leaving me with the ache between my legs, and only one way to satisfy it ...

But unanswered questions swam through my head. Why was I in a cemetery, kissing a man who can turn into a raven, when he still hadn't even told me what danger was hunting us? Was this kiss just another distraction so he didn't have to answer my questions? I tore myself out of the fantasy of Cole, and clamped my mouth shut, forcing his tongue out. My body screamed in protest, but I had to do it.

Cole pulled away, holding me at arm's length, his eyes boring intently into mine. His expression said he wasn't done with me, that he wanted more. I gasped for breath, forcing back my desire, stomping it down inside so I could *focus*.

"I knew you didn't know martial arts." He grinned wickedly, bending in to kiss me again.

And as I stared at him, and the heat raged through my body, I saw something I never expected to see. I saw Ethan.

In Cole's features, I saw the same look Ethan had given me hundreds of times, a look of desire. He *wanted* me, and being wanted by Cole felt so, so right. But in Ethan's case, that look had been a lie. *Cole is not Ethan, he's not the same.* I tried to tell myself, but I couldn't shake the horrible feeling I was walking into another trap. I was setting myself up to get hurt again.

"You look scared all of a sudden," Cole said, his voice throaty. He squeezed my shoulder. "Why? I'm not going to hurt you." I thought he would add *unless you like it* on the end of that sentence, but he didn't. At least for once he knew when to be serious.

"I don't know that." I stared at a spot just above his shoulder, focusing on the black smudge across a gravestone. If I looked him straight in the eye, I would lose myself again. "I don't even know *you*. I don't know what you are, what you're capable of."

Cole's eyes narrowed. "You sure can turn it off and on like a faucet."

His sharp tone cut through me. "I'm sorry—" I caught myself. "No, do you know what? I'm not sorry. You're kissing me in a cemetery, and I don't even know what's going on. I can't do this,

Cole. I can't get hurt again. I have to be able to trust you, and right now that's just not possible."

"You trusted me on the bike."

"That was different. You know what you're doing on that bike. I don't think you know what you're doing with me."

Cole squeezed my shoulder harder. "Fine. Ask your questions. If you're so desperate to know what's going on, what I'm capable of, ask me anything. I won't lie to you."

I took a deep breath, steadying myself. My pulse was still racing, the fire Cole's touch ignited still burning inside me. I forced myself to step back again, placing some distance between us. Cole didn't let go of my shoulder. "What did that note mean? Who was Harry?"

"You looked at that note? It was private."

"Of course I did. You weren't telling me anything!"

"Fine. Harry is Victor Morchard's son," Cole said. "And he's dead because Thomas Gillespie killed him."

"And why did Thomas Gillespie kill this Harry?"

"Because he heard I'd run away, and he wanted to punish Victor for letting me get away. So he killed Harry and drained his blood."

"That's sick."

"I don't disagree."

"Does this mean Thomas Gillespie arrived in Crookshollow early?"

"At the very least, he's in Loamshire. Harry took the train from Oxford into Crooks Crossing yesterday. He was heading home to the castle, so I guess he did that, inside a coffin. I saw him with my own eyes when I snuck out of your flat last night to go and investigate. Sir Thomas must have attacked Harry as he left the train station."

"In broad daylight?"

"Vampires can read minds and manipulate memories. Anyone who saw anything probably had their memories altered.

You see why I am so desperate to keep you away from these people. Thomas Gillespie is the most dangerous man you could ever encounter, Belinda. Even Victor Morchard was afraid of him. The stories Victor used to tell me..." Cole shuddered. "I sincerely hope that you never have the horror of making his acquaintance."

"But the Morchards think you are dead, and the Gillespies have had their revenge. So what's the problem? We just hide out for a few days until the Gillespies go away, and then find a way to break the bond. It will be fine."

"Ah yes. The problem," Cole said. "Is that Thomas Gillespie can read minds. And as soon as he arrives at Morchard Castle, Victor will probably offer him another of his Bran as payment for the debt, lest he lose another child. And as soon as Sir Thomas comes close to Byron – which he will no doubt do – he will *see* in Byron's mind that I am still alive, and he will see your shop. Sir Thomas will then kill my brother, and he will come for what is rightfully his. He won't have any qualms about killing you, either. Thanks to Byron sticking his nose in where it doesn't belong, we are all in great danger, unless I can figure something out."

My stomach tightened. "What can we do?"

"Your friend Ryan can help us, I think. If I can state my case to him." Cole swept his eyes around the cemetery. "But ideally, I need to figure out how to become a proper rogue. That's why I came here. Mikael's witch is going to leave me a message here if she finds someone powerful enough to break the curse. I don't see a message, but ... this cemetery has been the site of a massive magical onslaught. It's the only place I know of where rogue ravens have been in recent months. What went down here was so intense, I wondered if there were some way to capture the residual energy here, to harness it and somehow use it to break me free of my bondage."

I'd spent two days in the company of this man, and now hanging out in charred cemeteries talking about magical spells seemed perfectly normal. "And have you found anything?"

Cole sighed. "Unless you count a beautiful woman with no Kung Fu abilities who won't allow me to kiss her, I've found nothing. I don't really know what I'm looking for. This is magic beyond my knowledge. I'd need to speak to a witch. I don't suppose you happen to know any witches?"

I tapped the nearest grave with my foot. "I've got friends in low places."

He squeezed my shoulder. "You make me laugh. It feels so good to laugh."

"Yeah, I know what you mean." I stared down at his body, rigid beneath his leather jacket. It occurred to me I hadn't checked his leg yet today. "Hey, how is your wound?"

"A lot better, thank you. I can almost fly normally now."

"Yeah? Show me."

Cole looked concerned. His grip on my shoulder tightened. "You want to see me in my raven form again?"

"Yes, please." I suddenly needed, *desperately* needed, to know he was truly OK. *Is it because he's your only defence against these evil people? Or is it because you care about him?*

Plus, watching Cole transform into that beautiful, silken bird was seriously hot, but I didn't think I was quite ready to tell him that.

Cole turned away from me, facing up at the waxing moon, and gripping the edge of a nearby stone with both hands. He took a deep breath, and started to change, his body shrinking down into itself as his arms bent awkwardly, the black feathers sprouting from his skin and spreading over his body, shrouding him in midnight. When he turned back to look at me, he was perched on the edge of the tombstone, and his eyes were the only part of him that seemed connected to the human Cole, the one I knew, the one I'd just been kissing. Every other part of him was pure raven.

I pulled his clothes off the tombstone and balled them under my arm. Cole tapped the stone twice with his beak, then with another glance in my direction, he took off. He didn't get much higher than my waist before he half glided, half crashed on to the top of a headstone, losing a few tail feathers in the process. He turned around and glared at me, as if to say. "I meant to do that."

"Sure you did," I answered him, instantly feeling weird. Could he even understand me in his raven form?

Cole flapped from headstone to headstone, each time rising a little higher, flying a little longer. When he reached the end of the row, he doubled back, this time clearing the entire width of the cemetery in a single graceful swoop.

"That's it!" I cried, clapping as I watched him soar higher. "You're doing it."

Cole zoomed across the cemetery, moving in swift circles about my head. He moved so fast he was nothing but a black blur. A couple of times I lost sight of him as he swooped and dipped between the blackened trees.

With a self-satisfied "croak!", Cole soared back down and landed on the tombstone, gracefully folding his wings away. He tapped the stone again, then morphed back into his human form. His feathers slid back into his skin, his bones cracked as they rearranged themselves, and within a few moments I was standing opposite a very naked, very smug-looking Cole.

"Well, how did I look?" he asked, spreading his arms wide and giving me a very unrestricted view of ... all of him.

"Um ... you look great. I mean, you flew great. Nice and straight." I could feel the heat rushing to my cheeks. I tried to avert my eyes from his sculpted chest and the deep Adonis V that led my eyes straight down to ... "I particularly liked the barrel roll."

"Yeah, well. I've got a girl to impress." Cole smirked, and wrapped his powerful arms around my neck. I breathed in the scent of him, that woody, natural scent that drove my body wild.

'Cole ..." He was looking like he wanted to kiss me again, and I just couldn't handle it. "Please ..."

"Do you really want me to put my clothes on?" He asked gently, his lips an inch from mine. His breath sent a shiver through my body. My fingers itched to run all over his body, my tongue felt heavy, desperate to have his slide over it once more. I could feel his hard on through the thin fabric of my dress. All it would take was for him to lift up my skirt and ... the thought made my stomach turn with fear. *Not yet.* I wasn't ready.

"Belinda? Should I get dressed?"

No. "Yes."

Cole sighed, and backed away slightly, the spell between us broken. "Fine. Give me a moment. We'll go visit your friends, and see if we can't find a way out of this mess. And maybe then, you might consider allowing me to do all the naughty things I've been imagining since the day I met you."

I gulped. Damn, that was tempting. "We'll see."

11

BELINDA

*W*e rode back toward the village, and pulled into Holly Avenue, a beautiful tree-lined street in the nicest area of town. There were no terraced houses in sight – the whole street was lined by beautiful Tudor mansions and Regency manor homes. Raynard Hall dominated the entire view. A stately gothic manor, it was one of the grandest houses within the boundary of the village itself, although there were plenty of other manor houses and castles dotting the landscape of Loamshire county. The area wasn't just famous for witches, it's been a favourite haunt for the English nobility for centuries.

The iron gates had been left open for us. Cole tore down the drive, coming to a screeching halt in front of the tall doors. He swung himself off the bike and turned to help me. "I can manage," I mumbled as I tried unsuccessfully to swing my leg back over. My thighs had turned to jelly.

"Of course," Cole stepped back, watching me struggle over the heavy frame with an amused expression on his face.

I was still trying to disentangle myself from the bike when Alex opened the door. "Hey, you two." She descended the steps, wearing a beautiful strapless emerald dress that perfectly accentuated her bright eyes and stunning body. Cole had told me to dress for comfort, and I felt thoroughly inferior in my dusty jeans and grey jumper. I finally managed to swing my leg over and slide off the bike, using the handlebars to steady my shaking legs. A biker chick I was not. Alex embraced me, her familiar sweet perfume making me feel instantly at ease. Miss Havisham, her calico cat, wrapped herself affectionately around my legs.

"It's been a long time since I've seen you outside the bakery," she grinned. "And on a motorcycle, too? Who are you, and what have you done with my friend Belinda?"

I laughed, and jabbed my elbow in Cole's direction. "You can blame him for the bike. And trust me when I say I won't be getting one of my own."

Cole tucked a stray strand of black hair off his face. "She likes cuddling up close to me, is her problem."

I felt the heat rushing to my cheeks again. If Alex noticed, she didn't mention it. She stepped forward, her hand outstretched. "It's nice to meet you—" she started to say, but then Cole looked up at her, and Alex gasped.

"I recognise you," she whispered. "You were following Isengrim."

What? My face flushed again, but this time it was anger. Cole had told me Isengrim was a very bad wolf shifter, but he'd never told me he was acquainted with the guy. And now Alex was staring at Cole with terror in her eyes, I suspected it had something to do with the shifter war that erupted at Ryan's exhibition opening. *Is this some other secret that Cole's been keeping from me? He's secretly in league with some secret shifter society that had attacked my friends?*

Cole nodded. "Please," he said. "I need to talk to Ryan."

"If you're involved with Isengrim, you must understand I'm not going to let you anywhere near him ... how did you survive?"

"I wasn't at the cemetery," Cole said. "You have to understand, I'm have no loyalty to that crazy wolf. I'm glad he's gone. I was only part of Isengrim's pack to collect information for my master. I had no interest in taking part in his insane necromancy fantasies."

I stared at Cole, not certain whether to believe him, but Alex laughed. "I'm not sure I trust you," she said, "but you'll win some points for that remark. Ryan will soon cut your throat out if you're a danger to us. Come inside, both of you. Ryan's in the yellow drawing room. I can't even believe I'm living in a house with enough rooms we have to categorise them by colour."

Inside the grand hallway, Alex took our coats and hung them. I embraced my friend. "He's gorgeous," she whispered into my ear.

"Meow." Miss Havisham concurred.

"I know." I grinned back. "Hopefully he's legit. I'm worried that you recognise him from some dark event."

"Ryan will know," she grinned, and took my hand, leading us down a wide corridor lined with dark furniture and stuffy portraits in gilded frames. "Come on, it's through here. I'll have to lead the way. It's pretty easy to get lost in this place. I put a cup of tea down once my first week living here, and I still haven't found it."

I cringed. There is nothing worse to an English lady than losing a half-enjoyed cup of tea.

We entered a large room toward the back of the house. Unlike the other rooms we'd passed, this one was light and airy, with floor-to-ceiling windows along one wall overlooking a lush back garden. There were no ancient mahogany furnishings here, the room was painted a soft pastel yellow, with bright modern art adorning the walls and Scandinavian-style couches seated around a roaring fireplace. Ryan was sitting close to the fire, one leg crossed casually over the other, a glass of Scotch in one hand. He stood as we came in, and embraced me as if I were an old friend. Miss Havisham took the opportunity to settle herself down in his spot.

I'd met Alex's fiancé only twice before, both times at her exhibition openings. He was lovely, but slightly stiff. Here, he looked truly comfortable. I suspected it was all those years of being a recluse – he must have built a tender familiarity with these walls. Even though Ryan was in the public eye again, he still preferred to be in his home or wandering in the forest to going out.

"It's wonderful to have you here, Belinda. Cole," Ryan reached out his hand. "It's good to meet you."

"And you, sir." Cole shook his hand vigorously, his eyes locked on Ryan's. "It's an honour. You're quite infamous in my circles."

"Indeed." Ryan gestured for us to sit. I relaxed into the couch, enjoying the softness of the suede fabric. A butler hovering in the far corner sauntered over and offered me a glass of champagne, which I gratefully accepted. Cole sat next to me, his warm hand resting on my knee. Alex settled next to Ryan across from us. I noticed the table between us had been set with a platter of cheese, crackers and pate. My stomach rumbled at the sight of real food I hadn't had to bake myself, and I reached forward to cut myself a wedge of brie.

Cole cleared his throat. "I'll just dive right in here. I asked Belinda to arrange for us to meet because I know who you are, and I know you've already discerned what I am. I'm in some danger, and I've inadvertently put Belinda in danger, also. I don't have many people I can turn to, and when Belinda said you were a friend I thought perhaps you might be able to give me some advice. You have some experience with rogue Bran."

"Wait." I lowered my wine glass and leaned forward. "Ryan knows about rogues and Bran? How?"

Cole nodded, and so did Alex. "What's going on here?" I demanded.

"She doesn't know?" Ryan asked Cole.

"She knows about me, but not about you. I didn't think it was my secret to tell."

Ryan grinned. He set his glass down and stood up. Alex reached up and grabbed his wrist. "Oh, babe, don't."

"I hardly ever get to do this now," Ryan said to her. "Let me have my fun." He turned to me and grinned harder. "Are you watching?"

I nodded, leaning forward in case I missed anything. I had a suspicion I knew what I was going to see. Cole squeezed my knee.

Ryan's change started immediately. Like Cole, it was his nose that shifted first, growing out from his face. But instead of forming a long, hard beak, Ryan's face grew a thick snout. Tawny hair bristled from his skin, and his ears pulled back across his head, sprouting a covering of dark hair and growing into triangles.

Ryan collapsed forward, narrowly missing the glass table as he landed hard on the rug on all fours. He shuffled his shoulders down and shrugged himself out of his shirt. His torso twisted, becoming long and lean. His back legs bent up like a dog, and as he stepped out of the black jeans that fitted his human form like a glove. He no longer had hands or feet – instead, four small paws sank into the rug.

A few seconds more and any sign of Ryan the human had disappeared. The large fox looked up at me with gleaming, mischievous eyes. He gave a sharp bark, and then darted from the room.

Alex sighed, and bundled up the pile of clothes on the floor. "Excuse me," she said. "I'll go take these to him."

Alone with Cole now, I squeezed his hand back. "I can't believe my friend's fiancé is a fox shifter, and you didn't even tell me!"

"He's not just any fox shifter, either." Cole grinned. "He's a hero. That wolf Isengrim had amassed a pack of rogue shifters and was going to reveal the existence of shifters to the world, but Ryan stopped him."

"Ryan's against that?"

"All sensible shifters are against it. Humans vastly outnumber us, and contrary to what the stories say, we're not immortal. No one – except Isengrim – wanted a witch hunt, which is exactly what would happen if the world knew about shifters. Ryan wasn't just protecting the people of Crookshollow, he saved the entire shifter population. For that, he's pretty beloved."

"What happened?"

"Isengrim and his pack were in the cemetery, trying to raise an ancient demon to usher in a new age of shifter domination, or some such nonsense. But Ryan and Alex stopped him, and killed most of his pack in the process. Isengrim escaped, and showed up at Ryan's exhibition, where Ryan disposed of him in a rather cunning and ingenious way, while managing to keep the existence of shifters secret. It was quite the scandal in my world, although I suspect Harry's death is about to eclipse it somewhat."

Ryan and Alex returned a few moments later, holding hands and grinning. Thankfully, Ryan was once again human and fully dressed. He sat down next to Cole and the pair started talking quietly. I dragged Alex into one of the room's darker corners. "I can't believe this," I exclaimed. "Ryan is a total fox!"

Alex snorted, narrowly rescuing her champagne from going up her nose. "Oh, we're going to play that game, are we? You are absolutely *fowl*."

I burst out laughing. The champagne spread through my stomach, filling me with a warm sensation. I finished my glass, and the butler rushed over to refill it. "What are the odds that we'd both fall for shapeshifters?"

"Pretty high in Crookshollow," Alex replied, grinning. "There are lots of shifters here. But what do you mean 'we've both fallen for'? Are you dating this guy?"

"Um ..." I wasn't really sure how to explain. "I don't know. I don't think so. But he's sort of ... living with me at the moment."

"He's *what?*" Alex's nails dug into my arms. "Is that a good idea? Aren't you moving awfully fast?"

"It wasn't *like* that. I found him in the park in his raven form. He'd been injured, and I was going to take him to the vet. But then I discovered ..." I gestured to Cole and Ryan, who were involved in a deep discussion beside the fire. "So the vet wasn't really necessary. He just needs a place to hide out at the moment, and he's helping me out in the bakery in exchange for some space on the couch."

"And you haven't even—"

"I don't think he's interested." I mumbled, my face flushing as I remembered our kiss in the cemetery.

"Oh, he's interested," Alex grinned. "He was checking out your arse when you walked down the hall."

"Really?" I clamped my hand over my mouth, but there was no way Alex hadn't heard the enthusiasm in my voice. The memory of our kiss surged through my body, and I felt my cheeks reddening.

Alex shook my wrist. "Look at you, Belinda. You're all flushed. You are completely smitten for this guy."

"I'm not, really—"

"Hey, I'm not one to judge. But you have to be careful. Trust me when I say the shifter world is dangerous. And you have to be gentle with yourself. You've only just had your heart broken. Are you sure you're healed from all that?"

"It's been months since Ethan left. I'm ready again—" I gulped as a lump formed in my throat. "At least, I *want* to be ready. It would be nice to have some proof that all the guys in the world aren't scumbags like Ethan."

"I know things are worse at the bakery than you're making out. I can see it in your eyes, can hear the panic in your voice when you talk about money. All I'm saying is watch out that you're not adding more stress to your life – stress you can ill-afford – all for the sake of that winged beauty." Alex dropped my arm, and patted me on the shoulder. "Now, that's enough friendly lecturing for the night. Refill?"

"Of course." Alex topped off our drinks, and we joined the boys back beside the fire.

While we polished off the rest of the champagne and the cheese, Cole explained the full story of how he'd been sold to Thomas Gillespie, and how he had run away. But now that Gillespie had killed Morchard's son, and Byron had discovered where Cole was hiding, he was in real danger of discovery. He held up his hand, showing Ryan the hot, glowing ring that had turned his finger into a dark, splotchy mess. "And that's added to the fact that if I don't find some way to break the oath that binds me to my masters, in a few days time I will be the property of a dangerous vampire ... if the pain doesn't kill me first."

"I think we might be able to help you with both your problems." Ryan said, as Cole finished his story. "First, you are right – it is a certainty that Gillespie will discover you are still alive. I say we anticipate that, by going to him with an offer. I happen to know your new master. Sir Thomas is a regular patron of the Halt Institute. He owns six of my larger paintings, so I don't think I'll have a problem getting an audience with him, especially when he is in the Crookshollow area."

I was shocked. "You associate with this guy?"

Ryan shrugged. "He's never been more than polite and supportive to me. In fact, I'd go so far to say I can't imagine him stooping to such crass acts as you describe. But then, I'm not really an expert on vampires. I do, however, know how to speak Gillespie's language. I'll offer him £150,000 to buy your service. That's a pretty significant sum, even for a Bran. When he accepts, you'll belong to me, Cole, and I will grant you freedom. Would that be amenable to you?"

"That is beyond generous," Cole said, his voice hushed. "I ... I don't know if I can accept."

I gasped at the figure. "Ryan, you can't do that. It's too much money."

"I'm not one to put a price on a life," Ryan said, setting down his drink. The black-suited butler swooped in and collected the empty glasses, then returned with fresh scotch for Ryan and Cole. Ryan squeezed Alex's hand, and continued. "For the longest time, I was trapped in a prison of my own making. It took this lady here to make me realise that I shouldn't be hiding away, I didn't need to be afraid of what I was. And now that I am free, I don't think that any creature should live in servitude of another, no matter how long the tradition has lasted. Simon here has been our butler for decades, but he is not a servant. I pay him a salary, and he's free to leave any time, with my regrets." Simon nodded wordlessly as he offered Alex a selection of wines.

"It's too much," I said again, shocked by how casually he spoke of such a sum. That money would easily pay off my debts with enough left over to buy the shop outright, and Ryan was talking about the money as if he were giving Cole a tenner for a taxi fare. I gazed down at the exquisite Persian rug beneath my feet. I noticed the legs of the table next to my seat had tiny gilded feet. *I guess to someone as rich as Ryan, £150,000 is spare change.* I couldn't even comprehend that kind of a life.

"I want you to have it, Cole." Ryan said. "You should have your liberty."

"I am in your debt," Cole said seriously. "I will pay you back every cent."

"That's not what I want," Ryan replied. "All I want you to do is take your freedom and make something of it. Tell me, have you thought what you will do once you are free?"

Cole didn't hesitate. "I want to own enough land to create a bird sanctuary. A place where birds can be taken if they are sick or injured. There would be experts there who could treat and study bird flu, trauma injuries, *everything.* And scientists could use the facilities to study the birds, as long as they were humane. The sanctuary would be a non-profit, so that no one had to worry they couldn't afford care if they found a bird in danger. And, of course, we would be a safe place for Bran to come and get the care they need if their masters are too cruel to find them treatment."

I stared at Cole in surprise. He'd never mentioned anything like that before. I found it hard to imagine this hard biker running a bird sanctuary and raising charitable donations. Cole didn't meet my eyes. He was staring into the corner of the room, looking as if his mind were a million miles away. He had spoken about the sanctuary with such conviction, his passion clear in his voice. I wondered what had spurred that dream of his.

Clearly, there was more to Cole than I'd imagined. I turned over his hand in mine, my eyes trailing the body of a snake as it curled around his wrist and slithered along his forearm. My chest tightened. I was falling hard for this guy.

"That sounds beautiful," Alex said. I nodded in agreement. Cole shook his head, turning back toward us. He gave a little smile, as if he'd only just realised we could hear him talking.

"Do you think Gillespie will accept your offer?" Cole asked quickly, as though he were keen to change the subject.

Ryan grinned. "I'll make it quite clear that it isn't open to negotiation. Because of Isengrim's recent attempt on my life, I've gained a bit of notoriety among the shifter clans and packs in the area. Sir Thomas, being what he is, cannot help but know what I have done. He may be cruel, as you say, but he is old-fashioned. He will not risk exposure for his family if things got ugly." Cole nodded. "Plus, it is a very generous offer. If I make it seem as if I'd like to buy you for my own use, I'm sure I can make him agree."

"Thank you." Cole reached forward and shook Ryan's hand once more, clasping it in his as if it were precious. "You don't know what this means to me."

"Oh, I have some idea." Ryan tapped Alex's knee, then stood up. "It's settled. I'll call Sir. Thomas immediately and set up a meeting for his arrival. Then we can have supper. And I think the two of you should spend the night here. If what you suspect is true, and Byron knows where you've been hiding out, then you're better off not returning to the bakery tonight."

"I can still open in the morning, right?" I asked, panic rising in my stomach. A single day without opening could be a disaster.

"Of course. But Cole shouldn't go with you. Alex and I will help you in the store instead."

No. I couldn't have them there, not beautiful, successful Alex and her rich fiancé. I couldn't allow them to see what was really going on, how bad things had got. My cheeks flared with heat just thinking about it. "It's okay, really. I've been managing on my own for months—"

"But now you're not on your own anymore," Alex grinned. *Yes, I am. I have to be.*

"I think it's a wonderful idea," Cole said. He squeezed my knee. I glared at him.

"What are you doing?" I hissed in his ear. "I can't bring them there. They'll see my flat. They'll know that I'm broke—"

"So what? It's the truth. They're your friends, and damn good friends, too. I don't see why you haven't told them, why you don't want anyone to help you. You don't have to do it on your own, Belinda."

"Yes. I do."

"Well, this is the one and only instance where I don't give a fuck what you feel. You're getting help, whether you like it or not. Besides, what choice do you have?"

He was right. I couldn't very well refuse their help without having to explain why, and I had no good explanation on hand. I grabbed his hand, prised it off my knee, and shoved it back in his lap. "Fine," I said, forcing myself to smile. "Thank you."

"This means an early start, doesn't it?" Ryan asked.

"I usually get up at 3:30AM." Ryan winced. Alex patted his knee.

"We'll manage, I'm sure. Oh! We have something for you." Alex went to a cabinet on the far wall, opened a drawer and pulled out two pouches. "Ryan's mother made these for us when we were having our own problems. They're still charged with energy, so they should work for you, too."

"What are they?" I asked, picking up the pouch Alex dropped in my lap. She handed the other one to Cole.

"It's a protection charm. It will hide you from the Bran, and it should prevent them being able to hurt you."

"But how?" I opened up the pouch and inspected the contents. All that was inside was a small, blue crystal and a bundle of dried herbs. "Is it poisonous?"

"No, it's a spell. Ryan's mother Clara is a powerful witch."

I scoffed. "Are you telling me there are really witches now? It's not enough that I just learned the world is filled with shapeshifters, but now there are old ladies flying around on broomsticks and making potpourri bags that can save me from evil?"

"She doesn't fly around on a broomstick, but my mother is a real, bona-fide witch." Ryan said. "She can trace her heritage right back to the original coven here in Crookshollow, the one that was almost completely wiped out in the witch trials."

I remembered that I'd heard the name before. "Clara? Does she work at *Astarte?*" Ryan nodded. "She's the woman trying to help Cole track down someone to perform the spell to break his bond. She said it was beyond her abilities."

"Then it must be a pretty powerful spell, as not much is beyond Clara," Alex said. "You can ask Elinor about her. Clara helped her bring Eric back from the dead."

I paused then, remembering something in the papers about how Elinor's fiance – the musician Eric Marshell – had died. But it had turned out to just be some sort of publicity stunt. It had happened before we were friends, so I didn't really pay much attention at first. I wasn't big on celebrity gossip unless pastry was involved. And Elinor was always dismissive when I asked about Eric, so I usually didn't ask. I'd assumed he liked to keep things private, because he was so well-known. Was Alex saying that Eric had *really* died, after all?

Were *all* of my friends part of this secret underground world of magic? Was I the only one in the dark?

I looked up at Cole, who was smiling that wicked, heart-melting grin down at me. Heat flared between my legs. *I'm definitely not in the dark anymore.*

Alex squeezed my shoulder, her expression saying that she would talk to me about Eric later. "Please, take the charm. Trust me when I say that it could save your life one day."

I stuffed the charm into my purse. "Of course. Thanks."

Ryan stood, and drowned the last drop of his Scotch. "Well, now that we have a plan in mind, should we adjourn to the dining room? We might need to go to bed early, since we have a busy day tomorrow."

Alex rolled her eyes. "Don't remind me. A 3:30am start? I didn't even know there *was* a 3:30 in the morning."

I forced a grin. "Well, you're about to find out."

IN RYAN'S AIRY, beautiful dining room we sat at a table that seated twenty and had a beautiful supper of cold beef sandwiches and delicate lemon tarts (I made a note to ask that grizzly old butler – Simon – for the recipe), and finished off another two bottles of wine between us. Cole and Ryan entertained us with stories of their shifter lives, and we asked endless questions about what it was like being two different creatures inside one body. Miss Havisham took up residence on the window seat and glared at us with all the derision only a cat could muster.

The more I drank, the funnier Cole's stories become. My whole face hurt from laughing so much. It had been so long since I laughed. I was feeling giddy by the time Ryan looked at the clock and suggested we adjourn to bed. "I've made up some guest rooms for you," he said. "Simon will show you where they are. We'll see you bright and early in the morning, Belinda."

"It will be okay," Alex said, squeezing my shoulder. "You'll see."

"Yeah," I said, all my mirth fleeing my body with the reminder that tomorrow they would be privy to all the behind-the-scenes workings of the shop. Dimly, through the haze of alcohol, I wondered if maybe I could keep them from going upstairs. If they stayed in the kitchen and behind the counter, they might never figure things out.

Simon walked us silently to a guest wing on the west end of the house. Alex and Ryan had been working to redecorate several of the Hall's old-fashioned, dark rooms with their modern, bright style. This wing was still undergoing its transformation, and our journey took us past unplastered walls and cans of paint stacked haphazardly against the wooden mouldings. There was not a mahogany sideboard nor gilded portrait in sight.

Simon showed us two rooms opposite each other. Mine was painted a soothing pastel blue, with billowing curtains and a gorgeous view toward the edge of the forest. Cole's room was ultra-modern, with black and chrome accents and a view over the village. We thanked Simon, who nodded wordlessly and slunk back off into the depths of the house, to do whatever it was that butlers did when there was no one to wait upon.

And I was alone with Cole once more. He was standing in the doorway of his room, regarding me with that stunning, self-satisfied smirk that made my insides feel like pudding. The memory of our kiss earlier replayed in my mind. A surge of energy pulsed through my body, a white-hot current of desire. I wanted him to stay with me, to kiss me again.

But it was the wine talking. It was a bad idea. I wasn't ready. I wasn't over Ethan. Hell, I was still seeing his face around town. *I couldn't* ...

The energy reached my core. The ache between my legs was certainly going a long way to convince me I *was* ready after all.

But what about him? Cole didn't move closer to me. He regarded me from across the hall with his usual amused expression. I wished I could read what he was thinking, to sense if his heart was pounding against his chest, the way mine did every time we were alone together.

"Well," I said lamely, gripping the door handle of my room so hard my knuckles turned white. "It looks like things are going to work out."

"Yeah," Cole grinned wider. "It looks like." His hand gripped the doorframe, and he swung his body toward me. Cole was always so in control, it was so hard to tell when he was serious and when he just thought something was a game. I stepped back, trying to give myself space to think. *Fuck, I shouldn't have drunk so much...*

He smells so good.

Cole let go of the door frame and took another step towards me, closing the gap between us in a heartbeat. He leaned against my door, his head bent toward me, his eyes smouldering.

Did he really mean what he said earlier, about showing me what I meant to him? Did he feel what I felt when we kissed, that amazing electrical storm going off inside my body? Or is that just normal for him? Does he do this with every woman he meets? Does he want to kiss me right now? Why doesn't he kiss me?

"Belinda," Cole said, his voice coming out as a growl. Goddammit. That was so hot. *Should I kiss him? Can I do that? Oh god, he looks so good.*

"I have to go to sleep," I said, intending my words to come out sharply, to force him to back off, for both our sakes. But instead they came out in a husky whisper, almost an invitation.

"I know," he said, that stupid grin still plastered across his face. "You have lots of work to do in the early morning."

I nodded vigorously, like one of those bobble-head dogs. "So ... goodnight."

"Goodnight, Nightingale," Cole said, that smirk never leaving his lips. I made to step backward, but he grabbed my arms, and pressed his lips to mine.

The touch of him was like an electrical charge surging through my body. My limbs pulsed with heat, my whole face glowed with the sheer delight of his touch. His hands cupped my cheeks as he teased my lips open, pushing his tongue between them and stroking mine. He had the faintest taste of whisky on his breath. The taste of him drove me wild.

Giddy with wine and warmth, I leaned against him. There was no pulling back now. I was committed. My hormones were speaking for me. Electricity shot through my whole body, as if I'd stuck my tongue in a light socket instead of in his mouth. At first I felt nervous, knowing that Cole was so much more experienced than me. But then he moved his hands down my body, moaning against my lips as he pressed one palm into the small of my back, the other cupping my ass, pushing my body up against him. I relaxed into the kiss, my nerves beginning to dissipate as I succumbed to the deliciousness of his touch.

This felt so different from the kiss we'd shared at the cemetery. It was so much hotter, so much more urgent. That kiss had been exploratory, inviting. But this was passionate, obsessive. It melted away my doubts, obliterated my nerves. My whole body came alive for him, it ached for his touch in a way I'd never ached before.

Cole pulled away slightly, lightly biting my lip and causing me to let out another low moan. "Let's get you to bed," he grinned, as he pushed the door open and pulled me into my room.

That grin. Shit, it did things to me. My heart seemed to sink deeper into my body.

Once inside, Cole slammed the door behind me. "Now you

can't go anywhere," he whispered, his hand on my face again, entwined in my hair. "Now you are mine."

His words made my chest flutter. He sounded so certain, so sure. Cole wanted me, and he always got what he wanted. I was only too happy to oblige.

Cole's kisses became more furious, more possessive. His tongue danced over mine, creating a delicious warmth that spread out from my mouth, down into my chest. I dug my nails into his back, claiming my own piece of him.

His hands traced my entire body, stroking my shoulders, my arms, skirting over my thighs. He cupped my cheeks and pulled me up, thrusting his tongue deeper. I moaned against him, drowning in him.

"I thought you didn't want me," I whispered against him as he pulled me across the room, toward the bed. The room was so large, it was a very long way to go. Plenty of time for him to change his mind.

"Are you kidding?" Cole grinned wider, as he pulled my grey jumper over my head. "I've been crazy about you ever since I first laid eyes on you."

He looked like an excited kid who'd just come downstairs on Christmas day to find the stack of presents under the tree. No one had ever looked at me like that before, like I was a present waiting to be unwrapped.

Evidently, Cole didn't want to wait any longer for the unwrapping. He pulled down the straps of my singlet top, exposing my collarbone. He laid a trail of kisses along my neck, over the sensitive skin. I shivered with delight.

"Fuck, Belinda." He groaned against my skin. "I would take you right now, but I want this to be so good for you."

"Cole, you don't have to—" But the thought became lost in his kisses. My body ached so bad, and his touch felt so good. I wanted him to keep doing what he was doing and to throw me down and fuck me, all at the same time.

"No," he murmured against my skin, his lips shooting a shiver of desire straight through my core. "We have to take this slow. I don't want you to remember anything else. *Anyone* else. I only want to you remember me and what I can do to your body. I want to make you *feel* as amazing as you *are*."

Oh god. "You talk so good."

"You *taste* so good." He plunged his tongue into my mouth again.

Cole's touches became more urgent as his hands roamed everywhere, his fingers drawing lines of fire across my skin. He lifted my arms and pulled the top over my head, throwing it somewhere across the wide expanse of the room. I might never find it again. Not that I cared.

He cupped my breasts through my bra, tracing their edges with his fingers. So slow, so patient. I pressed my body forward, desperate for more. He obeyed, reaching around with a single hand and unclasping my bra. Clearly, he'd had a lot of practice. He threw the bra out into the nothingness of the room, then held me at arm's length, his eyes trailed hungrily over my body.

"Fuck, you're beautiful," Cole grinned. I grinned back. It had been so long since I'd felt desired, like I was worth any guy's attention. But looking into his gleaming eyes and wild, mischievous expression – like that same kid who'd just been told his Christmas present was having a sleepover in a candy shop – I was starting to believe it.

He cupped my breasts again, his fingers deftly moving over the surface, circling the nipples. His touch traced a line of fire over my skin. *It must have been way too long, because I don't remember anything ever feeling this amazing.*

Cole bent down, and took my nipple in his mouth. I gasped as his tongue slid over the sensitive bud. *Oh, he's good at this!* Wetness pooled between my legs.

He licked and suckled at my breast until I writhed against him. I twisted my fingers in his long hair, pulling his face against me, enjoying the view of his wet tongue sliding across my hard nipple. When he moved across to the other breast and dragged his teeth lightly against the tip of my nipple, my knees buckled, and I sank against him, my need pulling me under.

Cole threw me across the bed, and covered my body in his. His weight against me felt reassuring, safe. His mouth sought mine, his tongue sliding against mine with more urgency. I responded in kind, our mouths fusing together like they were made for each other.

I tried to reach around him, to circle his whole body with my arms, but he was too muscular. I settled for stroking my hands over his shoulders, across what parts of his back I could reach, revelling in the way his hard muscles moved beneath his skin. Finally, I could give in to my own desires. I trailed my fingers over his inked skin, admiring the way the pictures seemed to move as his weight shifted.

"What are you looking at?" Cole broke the kiss and stared down at me, his eyes worried. "Did I suddenly grow a third nipple or something?"

"I was admiring your tattoos," I said, my voice wavering as he nibbled on my earlobe.

"Really? I can think of a few more exciting things you could be admiring."

Cole laid a trail of kisses along my jawline. Every touch of his lips was like a little electric jolt. The tribal pattern on his shoulder danced as he moved his arm to cradle my head. His lips continued their trail down my neck, nuzzling into the small of my shoulder. The skin there sizzled with heat. As his lips touched it my body shuddered. He kept going, kissing along my collarbone, and down my chest.

I gasped as Cole drew my nipple into his mouth again, and that tongue swirled itself around the sensitive bud. A line of heat ran from his mouth right through my body, stopping between my legs, where the ache intensified. This was pure, exquisite torture.

Cole continued his slow, deliberate trail of kisses, moving over my stomach, his tongue plunging into my belly button. I was so turned on that when he kissed the edges of my underwear, my whole body convulsed. He grinned that wild, sexy grin. "Patience, Nightingale."

"Damn your patience!" I moaned, not even caring anymore how out of control I was, how desperate. I needed this so badly. I needed *him*.

"Just for that, you have to wait a little longer." Cole lifted my legs onto his shoulders and kissed my toes, behind my knees, each touch sending jolts of pleasure through my body. He ran his tongue up my thighs, squeezing my ass cheeks. He brushed his fingers over the material of my underwear, so lightly and delicately I could barely feel his touch. I growled in my throat and arched my back, trying to get him to touch me harder, to give me what I was aching for. But Cole simply grinned that infuriating grin, and went back to making circles on my thighs.

Finally, he hooked his fingers under the edge of my panties, and kissed a line across the top. I was so hot and wet by now, I was nearly ready to burst.

Slowly – agonisingly slowly – Cole rolled my underwear over my hips and down my legs, pulling my panties off my feet and tossing them from the bed. He leaned down and planted his soft lips on my mound, his eyes never leaving mine. That whisper of a touch nearly sent me over the edge.

Cole used his fingers to spread apart my lips, and he slowly licked the entire length of me, his tongue flicking over my clit before plunging inside of me.

All the surging energy inside of me concentrated on that one spot. Cole took his time, slowly licking and circling, unheeding to my groans. I bent my hips up toward him, begging him with my body to go faster, to let me give in to the rising orgasm that threatened to claim me, but he simply pushed my hips back down and went even slower.

"Ooooh, Cole, damn youuuuuuuu," I moaned, as he slowly circled me with his tongue. My body was on fire. I was burning in the flames of my desire. How did he do this to me?

Suddenly, Cole sucked my clit into his mouth and held it there, his tongue circling it like a propeller. He thrust a finger up inside of me, and I was gone. The fire consumed me, flames tearing through my body. I lost all sense of myself, all possession of my body. All that existed was the fire, the pleasure. My vision blurred, and turned red. The fire was everywhere, even inside my eyes.

Somebody was moaning, yelling, howling like a hyena. With a fuzzy mind, I realised that somebody was me. I should have felt embarrassed, but I was too far gone.

The flames burned up the last of me, and the heat slowly left my body. I relaxed against the sheets, my vision blurry, my whole body coursing with beautiful, quiet, heavenly bliss.

Wow. I'd had orgasms before, of course. And they were pleasant enough, but I'd never experienced anything like *that.* No one had ever made me scream or lose my sight before.

"Are you okay, there?" Cole leaned beside me, his breath hot against my ear as he made lazy trails across my stomach with his fingers.

"Mmmhmmm." He looked so smug, like he did this all the time. He probably did. But I didn't care. I'd never felt this good in my life. My body was a cloud, floating away. So *this* was what good sex was all about.

"I know you're pretty wiped right now." Cole licked my earlobe. "But I still have more in store for you."

"Mmmhmmm." His breath against my ear sent a shiver of delight through me. Cole circled his fingers around my nipples, teasing them into hard marbles once more. Despite the incredible orgasm that had completely wiped me of energy, I could feel the ache returning, my body responding to his touches. I was ready again. I wanted more.

Cole bent over me, his black hair brushing my cheeks as he kissed me again. This time, his kisses were more urgent. He was done playing with me, now we were both ready for him to be inside me.

"Belinda, you're so fucking hot." He grabbed my shoulders and rolled me on my side. I had no idea what he was doing, but I couldn't find the words to protest. Cole lay down behind me, pressing his body against my back, wrapping his strong arms around my body, his leg hooked over mine. His cock pressed against my thigh, hard as rock.

Cole found a box of condoms in the drawer beside the bed. He rolled a condom over himself, and lay back beside me, one arm under my head, the fingers delicately stroking my nipple. The other grabbed my hip and pulled my leg up, opening me up. I closed my eyes in anticipation, the ache within me burning to be full of him.

Cole slid his tip inside me, his lips closing around my neck at the same time. I sighed with pleasure at the sensation of part of him inside me. Cole took a deep breath, his fingers digging into my thigh, then he thrust himself all the way in.

He was so huge that at first I gasped with the pain of it. He buried himself deeper, and the pain faded, becoming a deep, satisfying sensation. From this angle, he was never going to get as deep as he could go, but still I felt stretched, completely full. God, it felt so amazing. Cole pulled out, and sighed as he thrust into me once more, his length sliding through my wetness with surprising ease.

I'd never had sex in this position before. It was so odd not being able to see him, to look into his eyes. I wondered why Cole had chosen it. It didn't seem it would be the best for him—

He reached over me, and pushed his fingers between my legs, finding my swollen clit and rubbing it with practiced ease. Now I understood why he'd chosen this position – his hands had free reign to roam over my body. The ache of an approaching orgasm swelled inside of me, driven by his exploring fingers and the sensation of him sliding inside of me.

Cole's teeth dug into my neck as he increased his speed, each thrust shifting my body forward against the bed. The sharp pain only intensified the ache between my legs. I gripped the sheets, trying to hold myself in place, to prevent him from fucking me right off the edge of the bed.

His fingers circled me harder. I felt the pressure building inside my belly. Each thrust sent me closer to the edge, literally and figuratively. His hardness swelled inside of me, filling me completely.

He dragged his teeth along my neck, and I was gone. I tossed my head back, my body shuddering as the orgasm washed over me. The fire shot through my limbs, and red welts appeared before my eyes. For a few moments, I lost myself to the sensation as the pleasure washed over me. And then I was back, my body soaked in sweat and the delicious smell of him.

Cole grabbed both my hips with his hands and pulled my body against his, a low growl escaping his throat. "I love feeling you come against me," he whispered in my ear, his hot breath sending a shiver through my body. I pushed back against him, meeting each powerful thrust with my hips, driving him deeper. I could feel another orgasm building as his cock stimulated.

"Cole, I'm going to ... I can't believe this ..." I was so close, so close. My core was ready to burst again.

He obliged, his fingers finding my clit again, flicking the swollen bud while he fucked me hard from behind. I turned my head up to look at him, and he claimed my mouth with his, our tongues entwining. I moaned against his tongue as the third orgasm rocketed through my body, my walls closing around his cock, his hardness driving deep inside of me.

A few moments later, I went slack in his arms. Cole grunted and pulled out of the kiss. "You're so fucking hot," he moaned. "I'm not going to last much longer."

I wanted to see his face as he came, to feel his own pleasure after what he'd given to me. I pushed back with my hips again, meeting each of his thrusts with my body, driving him as deep as I could. Cole's body tensed, his fingers digging into my thigh. He squeezed my nipple hard, and bit down on my neck again. I felt his cock go rigid, and with a final, desperate thrust, he came, pounding deep inside of me, a deep, guttural moan escaping from his throat.

He flopped back against the sheets, his arms around me going slack, his cock still buried inside of me. "Wow," he said, his lips brushing my neck. He reached down and pulled out of me, tying a knot in the condom and setting it aside. He slumped back down on the bed with a contented sigh.

"Yeah, wow." I rolled over on to my back, cupping his face with my hands, enjoying the way his hair fell over his face, matted slightly by the sweat of our bodies. Cole gazed at me with heavy-lidded eyes, his expression unreadable.

"What are you thinking?" I asked, stroking his cheek.

"You should never ask a man that. It's always something filthy. Especially when that man has a beautiful woman lying naked next to him. Why, what are you thinking?"

"That this is nice."

"Nice? Nice? I give you three orgasms and all you can say is nice?" He rolled over so he was on top of me, pinning my body to the bed. He blew a raspberry on my skin, right over my collarbone. He pinned my arms with his shoulders and tickled me under my arms. I screeched as I broke down into uncontrollable spasms. "I'll show you *nice*."

"Cole! No, arrrggggh! I'll behave. I promise!" I gasped.

He stopped tickling, but he didn't climb off me. He grinned down at me, black ringlets flopping over one eye. "No, don't do that. I like you when you're misbehaving."

"I like it, too."

"You are getting under my skin, woman." he growled.

I grinned back, my chest swelling with pleasure at his words.

You're getting under my skin. Cole rolled off me and pulled me to him, placing his arm over me. His warmth seeped into my skin, I realised with a sinking heart that I was allowing him to get under my skin, too. I spent so much time assuming he wasn't interested in me, that I hadn't really considered what would happen, how I would feel if we did fall into bed together.

Well, it had happened. And I felt happy. And *that* made me scared. Terrified. This was a guy who belonged to a very different world, one that was currently trying to kill him. As much as I told myself that this was just about sex, about me having a positive memory of a guy who wasn't Ethan, I couldn't shake the feeling that I was falling for Cole. And that was a very, *very* bad thing to do.

12

COLE

*W*e slept for a time, Belinda's face resting in the crook of my arm, her beautiful body stretched around mine like a reposing cat. There was a moment, just after we'd collapsed together, where a worried look came over her lovely face, and I thought for sure she was going to bolt. I was surprised by the depth of the ache in my chest at the idea of her leaving. I held her extra tight and whispered something filthy in her ear, and that seemed to convince her to stay.

My mind flickered in and out of consciousness, filled with pleasant dreams where Belinda and I floated on clouds, rolling naked together, our bodies pressed against each other. Her kisses tasted like warm bread fresh from the oven, her eyes danced with fire, her body shuddering with pleasure whenever I touched her. The pain in my finger faded into oblivion.

I opened my eyes, and realised that part of the dream was real. I was kissing Belinda, in a bed so soft it might have been a cloud in another life, and I was hard again.

Her tongue slid over mine, her hands kneading my shoulders. Her kisses were languid, sensual, half-cloaked in sleep. I returned her touch, wrapping my body around her and pressing her into the sheets.

This is the best way to wake up.

As if reminding me that my situation was precarious, pain flared through my body, starting in my swollen index finger, and moving along my arm, across my chest. I kissed Belinda harder, forgetting the pain in the warmth of her lips.

I pulled myself on top of Belinda, spreading her legs wide. I rolled another condom on and thrust into her in one deep stroke, enjoying the way her warmth slipped around me, sheathing me entirely. Her lips parted ever so slightly, and she sighed with pleasure as I slid up into her, grinding my thighs against hers, pushing myself deeper than I had the night before. Sometimes women were frightened to take in all of me, but not Belinda. She accepted everything I had to give.

I cupped her head in one hand, the other gripping her curvaceous ass, and pushed her body up to meet mine. Belinda wrapped her knees up around me, angling her hips to allow me to go deeper. *Yes.* I pounded into her, relishing the way her eyes locked on mine, fully losing herself in the moment.

Getting an idea, I pulled her knees forward, placing her feet on my shoulders. Not many girls had the flexibility to do this position for long, but Belinda sighed with happiness as she pulled my head down with her knees and I slid even deeper into her. Her sighs quickly turned to moans as my thrusts stroked her in just the right way, my pelvic bone hitting her clit while my cock rubbed that special spot deep inside her.

"Oh, Cole." She breathed through gritted teeth, her black hair bouncing wildly around her face. I loved it when she said my name. "Oh, oh!"

I continued to thrust steadily, enjoying the view of Belinda's head tossing about wildly and her lips parting as she panted in pleasure. I could feel myself getting closer, the tension in my body pulling me under. There was nothing in the world I wanted more right now than to come inside this beautiful woman. But I had to hold on a bit longer, for her.

I had to make her forget that fucking loser ex of hers. And the best way to make someone forget is to fuck the memory out of them.

I gritted my teeth and slowed my pace, concentrating on meeting Belinda's gaze, on keeping my eyes locked on hers. I leaned against her, pushing her knees along my shoulders, and manage to press my lips to hers. As I kissed her, I felt her lips tremble against mine. She was close.

"Belinda," I whispered against her lips.

Belinda's walls tightened around me, squeezing my cock inside her. She threw her head back and moaned as she came, her orgasm sending pulses of delight through her entire body. She shuddered against my cock, and I was so close that sent me over the edge. I felt myself go rigid, and then my own orgasm claimed me. I grunted as I pounded into her one final time, relief spreading through my whole body as a hot wave of pleasure rose up and washed over me.

I leaned back, allowing her to slide her legs from my shoulders. I took care of the condom, then curled up next to her, wrapping my body around hers and pulling her against me. I loved the feeling of her soft skin against mine. Usually I wasn't keen on all the cuddling women liked after sex, but with Belinda ... I couldn't get enough of the feel of her.

"I could do this all night, in every conceivable position," I said, running my fingers along the edge of her breast. Belinda shuddered as the last vestiges of her orgasm fluttered through her body.

"I have to work in a few hours," she murmured, her eyes flickering shut. "Bread must be baked, Eccles cakes iced ..."

"Then you should sleep. I'll try to keep myself from further devouring you until tomorrow night, but then you are mine."

"Mmmmmhmmmm." Belinda didn't open her eyes. A few moments later, she was breathing steadily, her chest rising and falling with a regular rhythm. She had this enormous smile on her face that made my chest feel tight, and not from the pain that shot periodically through my body.

This night had been amazing. Belinda's body was even more incredible out of her clothes. I had been so worried she would be afraid of sex, after what her scumbag ex had done to her, but from the moment I kissed her she was completely uninhibited. Behind her sugary-sweet exterior there was an inner minx just dying to get dirty. And I was definitely keen to help her with that.

But now that I had satisfied her, the time for play was over. The night stretched out before me, and as I lay in bed I grew more restless. I thought of Byron, and of the way I'd acted when he surprised us in the forest. I probably shouldn't have been so rude to him, but I hated that he'd caught me off-guard.

We had a pretty shitty relationship. Growing up, our father had played us constantly against each other, and Byron usually came out on top. After father was killed, Byron wanted nothing to do with me. He spent all his time with Pax and Poe, learning to fight and drink and barrel-roll and all the things teenage boys did when they were mad at the world. And when our mother died ... well, we were never going to forgive each other for *that*. But even though Byron was a complete shithead, he was right – I'd taken too many stupid risks, and I wasn't being careful enough. I fucking hated it when Byron was right.

I should probably find him. We need to sort this out. If I got Byron killed, I'd never be able to forgive myself.

I inched my arm out from beneath Belinda, checking to make sure she was still asleep. I slid out of bed. There was a window on my side of the bed that overlooked the forest. I pushed it open, letting in a gust of cool air. Next, I put the charm Ryan had given me around my neck. Luckily, it was light enough that it wouldn't affect my flight too much. Neither Belinda nor I had bothered putting any clothes on again, so at least I didn't have to worry about that. I saw her charm looped around her wrist, and thought about taking it for Byron. But I didn't want to leave her unprotected.

I shifted as quickly as I could into my raven form, and hopped up on to the windowsill. I didn't want to leave the safety of Raynard Hall, but I had Byron to think about. We may have a difficult relationship, but he was still my brother, and I knew he'd be close by, watching for me.

It didn't take me long to find him. He was sitting on the top of the wrought-iron gate that barred the main entrance to Raynard Hall. I fluttered down and perched beside him.

You followed me here, I said to him in caw-tongue.

Of course, was his reply. *But there's some kind of magical field around the estate. I can't cross it.*

Raynard likes to keep the place free of vermin.

Byron scowled. *This isn't the time for your abrasive humour, Cole. What's that around your neck? You look like a carrier pigeon.*

It's a protective charm. It should shield me from detection. I'll see if I can get one for you, too.

Byron inclined his head. It was as close to a 'thank you' as I would ever get. *So you went to the fox? That's a pretty bold move.*

I did. And he's going to help us.

Us? You mean you're acknowledging that I'm part of this, too?

That's what I said, isn't it?

Such anger in one so young. Go on, Cole. Tell me what the fox plans to do.

I explained Ryan's idea to Byron, and also about the charm I wore. He didn't speak for some time, and then he nodded slowly, his beak dipping. *That is a good plan, but I see one flaw. You should know that Thomas Gillespie has already arrived. Pax saw them at Crooks Crossing this evening. They're hiding in the crypt beneath the old church. If he finds me before Raynard arranges this meeting—*

Caw tongue doesn't have a word for "fuck", so I just knocked my head against the gate a couple of times. Byron snorted.

Don't be dramatic. Just keep yourself hidden until Ryan can talk

*him into the trade. And if you could hide me too, that would be
appreciated.*

I stared at him in shock. *You would go rogue?*

*I don't really have a choice now, do I, little brother? Now, can you
get me past this barrier so I can hide inside with you?*

You know we can't go inside just yet. We have to know, *Byron. Our
only weapon is the knowledge of what he's up to. We have to know
what he's doing. Why does Sir Thomas even* want *a Bran? That's what
I don't understand. I have a feeling that's the key to this whole thing.*

Fine. I'll go. You stay here and I'll report back.

As if I'd trust you with something this dangerous. Let's go together.
I spread my wings and soared away over the village, trying to
keep my balance with the charm around my neck and the pain
flaring through my wing and my injured leg still dragging. A few
moments later I heard the flap of Byron's wings behind me.

We flew to Crooks Crossing in silence, darting high over the
forest – where any Bran on patrol would be unlikely to spot us –
and then dove low to cross the river that surrounded the next
village. The old church was easy to find. It dominated the tiny
high street of the village. The only other municipal buildings
nearby were a pub, a post office, and a hall covered in graffiti. A
couple of hoodlums with skateboards and cigarettes dangling
from their mouths loitered in front of the hall. Otherwise, the
place was dead and silent.

After doing a circuit of the churchyard to make sure there
were no Bran or other creatures on guard, we swooped down and
landed on one of the gravestones. I turned my head toward the
church. I could hear voices inside. I gestured for Byron to follow
me, and together we hopped down from the stone and dashed
across the grass toward the side of the building. We fluttered up
to the sill and peered through a stained glass window. I couldn't
see any lights inside, and it didn't seem to be where the voices
were coming from, either.

Down there. Byron pointed to the wall below us. There was a small window at the back of the garden, right down by the dirt. Behind it I could see the faint light of a candle flickering. We fluttered down and peered inside.

We were looking into a small crypt. I could see niches in the walls marking ancient tombs. In the middle of the room stood a dais upon which sat a stone sarcophagus. The elaborate carvings on the tomb depicted a warrior, possibly a local saint. He held a sword across his chest, and cherubs lounged on clouds around his feet. The lid had been tossed off the tomb, and it lay on an angle across the stone box, giving us a view of what lay inside it. I leaned closer, peering into the gloom, desperate to see for myself, and yet dreading what I knew I would find.

Inside the open tomb lay Sir Thomas Gillespie.

Beside me, Byron stepped back, his tail twitching. I didn't blame him. My chest was tight, all my senses on high alert. I didn't like being here, either. This was highly dangerous. Seeing Sir Thomas' serene face staring up out of that coffin brought it home to me. At any moment Gillespie might wake, and he'd sense our presence, and we'd be dead.

But, as I'd said to Byron, we were the ravens, the watchers. We needed to see, to *know*.

I don't even want to know what they did with the remains of that medieval knight. Byron said, shuddering.

Knowing Gillespie, he probably ate them. I replied, leaning in to peer at the rest of the crypt. It was probably early for him to be in bed, (as vampires tended to keep nocturnal hours because it meant less time in the presence of the sun) but he'd spent days on the road, so he must've been tired. Gillespie didn't need to sleep in a coffin inside a dingy crypt like some bad horror film trope. He would have occupied the best hotel suite in all of Loamshire. But coffins and crypts were part of his species' mythology, and Gillespie was the kind of vampire who took mythology very seriously. He liked to do things old school.

At the foot of the coffin sat Gillespie's two human servants;

Leonard and Rudolpho. They passed a bottle between them and argued over a card game they played by candlelight. Two rapiers and a shiny pistol leaned against the side of the tomb, within easy reach should anyone threaten their master.

Gillespie retained a purely human staff, partly for the ease of feeding (a vampire of the old traditions could feed from the same victim for many years without killing or turning that victim. It just took a lot of self-control.) and partly because Gillespie honestly believed that his kind were superior to shifters in every way, and especially to the Bran. To them, we were wild, feral creatures, lower life forms born to be controlled by humans and therefore undeserving of his interest. Sir Thomas would rather have no servant than resort to employing a Bran, even with our unique abilities.

Which was why it was so strange that Gillespie suddenly wanted a Bran. And why I was determined that it was not going to be me. For all the evil Morchard had done – and there had been plenty of that – it had nothing on what that peaceful face below me was capable of.

We shouldn't be here. Byron said, moving further away from the window.

We're here now, I hissed back. *There must be a way we could hear what they're saying.*

I inched closer to the window, flattening my body against the ground as much as possible, trying to stay in the shadows. The pain flared through my wing, pulling at me, trying to drag me back to my master. It was getting worse, the pull so intense at times that I inched backward toward the castle, before catching myself. I only had a day or so left before it overran me completely.

Don't think about the pain, I admonished myself. *Concentrate.* The vault walls were thick, but I had the hearing of a predator. Even so, I could only catch snatches of the conversation.

Cole, be careful! Byron hissed, jumping back from the window. *You're getting too close.*

"... the Bran's alive ... Mikael helping ... take care of ..."

Mikael.

I don't know how they knew, but they'd found out I was still alive. And if they were talking about Mikael, they must have known he had helped me hide from Morchard. They might assume Mikael knew more about my disappearance then he really did. They would try to get information about me out of him, and their methods would not be pleasant.

My chest tightened with fear. I had to warn Mikael as soon as possible. Not even his master would be able to protect him from Gillespie's wrath.

"... did you see something move ... window ..."

Shit. I peered through the grimy glass. Rudolpho got to his feet, grabbing the pistol and descending. A moment later he emerged around the edge of the church, his head darting from side to side as he searched among the graves for trespassers.

Cole, get out of there. Fuck! Byron screamed. He took off, soaring across the cemetery, heading for the thick cover of the forest that bordered the churchyard.

Byron, you idiot.

Rudolpho turned toward the noise, and saw the crow flying toward the trees. "Fuck!" He cried. "Leonard, come quick. One of the fuckers has been spying on us."

I heard footsteps as Leonard raced up the stone steps of the tomb and joined his brother in the grass. They darted between the stones, heading toward the edge of the forest. Rudolpho gestured to the tops of the trees, pointing out where he'd seen Byron enter the trees.

I crouched low, hiding as close to the shadowy church as I could, waiting for my chance. They were too busy looking in the trees to think about the window. As soon as the two men ran past my hiding spot, I unfurled my wings and took off, my heart pounding. I headed for the trees as fast as I could.

"There's another one. Get it!"

A shot rang out behind me. I squawked in terror, certain at any moment I'd feel the bullet biting into my skin. But I kept on flying, my injured leg twinging as I wrenched my body sideways. They had missed. Wind rushed through my feathers. I'd never flown this fast in my life. I cleared the treeline just as a second shot rang out.

The darkness closed around me, and I had to weave and dodge to avoid the branches crisscrossing in front of my path. Beady eyes regarded me from the gloom – the nocturnal birds watching me delve deeper into their territory. Anything to get away from Gillespie's servants and their gun.

Byron, where are you?

I heard wings flapping to my right. I looked down, and was relieved to see Byron flying along beneath me, his black body swooping gracefully, completely unscathed.

That was close, he said.

Too close. I replied, narrowly missing a large branch. This was the longest I'd flown on my injured leg, and it was really starting to give me trouble. *You're an idiot. If you hadn't have flown up when you did, they wouldn't have seen us. They will guess it was me spying on them.*

Probably. But it's too late, Cole. You heard those two idiots talking; they know you're alive. What are we going to do now?

We exited the forest and flew toward Crookshollow. There was no one, or no thing, following us. As we flew through the town centre, I glanced down at the clock on the top of the Halt Institute building. It read 3:06AM. *I have to get back to the house,* I said. *Belinda's going to be getting up and opening the bakery soon. I need to be there when she wakes up. As soon as they've left the house, I'll go warn Mikael.*

It's too dangerous. They'll be expecting one of us to go to Mikael. They'll ambush us. I'll go.

No, Byron. You need to go back to Morchard before he misses you. Right now they don't know you're involved, and we need to keep it that way as long as possible. This is my mess, and I won't get you killed for it.

You know, for an annoying brat of a brother, you're actually alright.

Thank you for that heartfelt compliment. I swooped in low as we turned on to Holly Avenue. The iron gates of Raynard Hall towered over the street, and I knew that behind them was Belinda, tucked up safe in bed, certain I was sleeping beside her. *Now get out of here.*

I have nowhere to go, remember? Byron growled. *Thanks to you.*

Fine. Wait here. Just give me twenty minutes to say goodbye to Belinda and make sure everything's organised with Ryan, and then I'll be back.

Don't worry, Byron called after me. *I'm not going anywhere.*

I sighed. *That's what I'm afraid of.*

13

BELINDA

I woke up to the sound of my alarm ringing. I reached across to the stack of books to shut it up, but my hand grazed only rich silk sheets. I fumbled around in the dark, searching for the edge of the bed, but instead of my makeshift bedside cabinet, there was a *real* cabinet, made of some kind of hardwood, holding a designer lamp and an iPod speaker.

I rubbed my eyes, and realisation dawned on me. I remembered now. I wasn't in my dingy flat at all. I was in a guest room at Raynard Hall that was more opulent than any hotel I'd ever stayed in, and I'd spent the night with Cole.

Cole...

I rolled over, but his side of the bed was empty. The sheets felt cold, and on the edge of the bed I found two small, black feathers. I crawled across the sheets and pushed on the window above his side of the bed. It swung open easily. *Odd.* I distinctly remembered locking all the windows last night, while Cole was in the shower. I didn't want anything unsavory to fly in.

Cole hadn't been in bed for some time, and wherever he'd gone, he'd done so in his raven form. But what had happened? Why had he left?

I squeezed my eyes shut. Was it me? Did last night not mean to him what it did to me?

I heard a knock at the door. I pulled the blankets up over my body. "You can come in," I called out. "But in the interests of full disclosure, I'm not wearing pants."

"I'm glad to hear it."

My heart pounded with joy at the sound of Cole's husky voice. He wasn't gone after all. He entered the room backwards, the bottom half of his body wrapped in a towel. I could just make out the wing of one of his raven tatts swooping down his lower back. In his hands he carried a tray.

"Simon left this outside the door," he said, as he set it down over my lap. I peered over the tray. It contained toast and eggs, sausages, bacon, mushrooms, a glass of orange juice, and a plate containing two of the lemon tarts from last night. There was a folded note next to them. I opened it up – it was the recipe.

"I want a butler so bad," I grinned, as I pulled the tray toward me.

I usually wasn't that hungry when I first woke up, but the smell of bacon and eggs overwhelmed me. I scoffed down the whole plate like I hadn't eaten in years.

"We'd better hurry if you want to get to the bakery in time." Cole glanced at my phone, then started to pull on his pants.

"Cole, did you go somewhere last night?" I asked.

"No, why?"

"There are some black feathers on your side of the bed."

"Really?" Cole glanced down at where I pointed. He picked up the two feathers and tossed them into a nearby rubbish bin. "Sometimes I shift during my sleep. It can be a bit hard to control, especially when you're unconscious. I bet that's what happened here."

"Oh, okay." That made sense. I let out a breath I didn't realise I was holding. It was fine. Cole wasn't lying to me. I set the tray aside and started to pull on some clothes. "I won't see you at the bakery today?"

He shook his head. "It's not safe. I'll hide out here, do some research into rogue Bran, see if I can find something useful in Ryan's enormous library, in case his plan doesn't work. Ryan and Alex are going to help you. They'll be watching out for you if anything happens or anyone shows up who shouldn't. Remember, don't wander away, and don't speak about Morchard or Gillespie to anyone. Can you do that?"

I nodded vigorously. "Of course."

"Good girl." He kissed me, his tongue running over mine. "Mmmm, much as I'd like this to continue, you really have to go."

I let the kiss linger for a few more moments, then finished dressing and dashed downstairs. I wished we could stay in bed all day, having more of that incredible sex, but it was more important to keep Cole safe. Alex and Ryan were already waiting in the cavernous entrance hall. Alex clutched a giant coffee thermos and a look of utter despair. "I hate you," she grumbled as I swung down the stairs. "There is no logical reason to get up this early."

"There is if you have loaves to raise," I grinned. Miss Havisham strutted into the entrance hall, greeting us with a wide yawn and a stretch of her lithe body.

"I've left instructions with Simon to contact Gillespie and set up the meeting," Ryan told Cole. "You don't have to worry about a thing."

Cole looked over at me, his eyes intense. "I have many things to worry about right now," He said.

"I won't take my eyes off her."

"Thank you." Cole shook Ryan's hand warmly.

Cole swept me into his arms and gave me one last, lingering kiss. Then he helped me into Alex's car, shutting the door behind me. We turned in the drive and I watched from the back window as Cole's figure grew smaller and smaller, until he was invisible against the dark sky.

Stay safe, my raven boy.

It was only when we were speeding along the high street towards the bakery that I realised I'd forgotten to ask Cole about the window.

"Are you sure Cole's going to be okay by himself?" I asked Ryan as I unlocked the store.

Ryan nodded, a strand of his red hair falling over one eye. Now that I knew he was a shifter, I was noticing him a lot more. He was beautiful, his face strong, his lips full and kissable, his eyes penetrating. A line of stubble ran along the edge of his jaw, and with his red hair all tousled, he channelled the spirit of his cunning fox altar ago. I wondered if it was part of the appeal of shifters, the way they looked a little wild, a little dangerous. "He can look after himself, I'm sure. Cole is a smart guy, if a little headstrong."

"A little?" I laughed, as I managed to twist the door open. "Here we are. Cole and I did a lot of the prep last night, so there's not really too much to do. We've got to get the loaves in the oven and ice the Chelsea buns and—"

The door slammed against the wall with a heavy THUD. I stood in gape-mouthed horror as I surveyed the scene in front of me. Tears sprung to my eyes when I saw what had been done.

The store had been completely trashed. The tables and chairs were overturned, many of them had been broken in two, the legs in splinters, utterly irreparable. The glass display counter had been smashed, all the shelves broken, and the cakes inside thrown against the walls. They'd pushed the coffee machine from the counter, and it lay in a mangled heap on top of a pile of smashed crockery. I could see that every item on the kitchen shelves had been swept on to the floor, and the doors of the oven torn off and bent in the middle. And in a final act of vicious hatred, someone had opened all the milk and cream cartons from the fridge and overturned them, so the whole place was covered in a sticky, milky film that was already beginning to smell.

No.

Chairman Meow sat on the counter, licking up a puddle of milk as it leaked from one of the overturned cartons. He looked up and gave me a pitiful meow, as if to say, "I didn't do this! I'm just making hay while the sun shines."

"Belinda ..." Alex's voice caught in her throat.

Oh, no.

I blinked once, twice. I hoped dimly that I was dreaming, that this was some horrible nightmare, and soon I would wake up in the big, soft bed in Raynard Hall, with Cole's strong arms around me, the scent of him still clinging to my skin. But when I opened my eyes again, there was no Cole, no soft bed, no lovely modern bedroom. There was only the ruins of my beautiful bakery.

The nightmare was real.

I took a step into the room, my heart plunging down to my feet as I kicked aside splinters of tables and chairs. They were only good for firewood now. I could make a bonfire of my hopes and dreams. And as I picked up Chairman Meow off the counter and held him to my chest, I realised with a hard feeling in my heart that I knew who had done this.

"Ethan," I whispered, the tears spilling down my cheeks. He'd done this, I know he had. There wasn't anyone else who could possibly have hated me this much. I thought back to the other day when I thought I'd seen him on the street. I'd chalked it up to my mind playing tricks on me, but I was wrong. It had been real. Ethan had returned to take the last piece of my life from me.

"I don't think it was your ex." Ryan stepped forward, and from the debris he picked out a large, black feather. "This belongs to a Bran."

"But who? And why?" I sniffed, burying my cheek into Alex's

shoulder. Staring at that long black feather made me feel sick. If it wasn't Ethan, than what had happened here?

"My guess is, it's one of Morchard's servants. They must have found Cole here, and decided to pay him a visit. You're lucky you weren't here last night." Ryan held up the feather, turning it around in the light. "This was left here deliberately. It's a message."

"What does it mean?" Alex asked.

"It means, 'Stay away from Cole, or else.'"

14

COLE

The charm around my neck weighed me down, restricting my ability to soar high or manoeuvre through tighter corners. But it was worth it if it kept my movements invisible from my pursuers.

It was such a stupid risk to go out again while the sun was rising, knowing that both Sir Thomas and Morchard were probably looking for me. But I owed it to Mikael. The Carnarvons lived in a beautiful Hall on a sprawling estate just outside of Crooks Crossing. I'd visited the estate several times in my life with my master. Even though the Morchards and Carnarvons detested each other, they had an alliance of sorts when it came to protecting their own affairs, and it was important to make a show of gentility for society. But neither family would travel to the other without a Bran for protection. That was how Mikael and I knew each other.

We were supposed to be enemies, but when I looked into his angry eyes, I saw the same distaste for servitude I knew burned in my own. Perhaps the other Bran suspected something, for we were never allowed to speak to each other. But when our bitter eyes met across the room at a ball or garden party, I knew I was communicating with an ally.

The first time we spoke, Mikael brought me the news of my father's death. He risked punishment by leaving his post to find me. I never forgot what he'd done, but it was not long before I had to return the favour.

Mikael's younger sister was born with a strange deformity. She couldn't fully shift from her raven to human form. Each time she tried she became stuck in a strange half-human, half-bird state, her limbs deformed painfully and her skin itching with half-grown feathers for days before she reverted back to her bird form.

A Bran that couldn't shift into human form was basically useless, so the Carnarvons loaned her to Victor Morchard, to see if he might be able to put her to good use in the aviary. He was planning to conduct experiments on her, the same kind of experiments he'd performed on my mother.

Two years ago, Mikael had come to me while I was out on patrol, begging me to help him get her out of the aviary. 'But what's the point?" I argued with him. "She'll still be your master's property. He can just send her back here again. Her only option is to go rogue, but then, how does she break the bond?"

"I know all this," Mikael's beady eyes blinked furiously. "But I have to do *something*. I can't just leave her in there to be poked and tortured. Maybe I can find a witch to help me break the bond, so we can both go rogue together. There are still plenty of witches in Crookshollow. But to do that, she needs to be free of your master's cage first."

I thought of my mother trapped inside that thick cage, too sick to move, to attempt an escape. She probably didn't feel a lot of what my master did to her. But Mikael's sister was perfectly healthy, apart from her strange disability. She would be able to assist in her own escape. Which meant we had a chance.

"Fine," I said. "I'll do it."

We engineered a pretty daring plan. I stole a pair of gardening shears and every night when I came back from patrol, I cut a few small wires on one low corner of the aviary. After two weeks we had a large enough hole to sneak in and out of. Next, I managed to procure a glass cutter. One day when the Morchards had some workmen over to lay concrete to extend the patio, I snuck around the aviary and, my deed hidden by the noise of the concrete mixer, cut away a section of the glass just large enough for a raven to fit through. I hid the hole with a potted plant, and dumped the glass cutter in the workmen's lorry.

Meanwhile, back at the Carnarvon's, Mikael created a diversion and snuck away. He met me over Crookshollow forest, and we swooped into the estate, crawled through the hole and pulled his sister out, replacing her body with a dead raven we'd found in Fauntelroy Park. Morchard would never know the difference.

Mikael took her to a witch he'd found. She knew the dark rite that would free a Bran from his or her servitude. We begged her to perform the same rite on all of us, but she said it stripped her of her power, and she would only do it once. We had to leave his sister there, and return to our lives of servitude.

Mikael's sister was free, and her secret would remain safe as long as she went far away from Crookshollow. She spoke a tearful goodbye in caw-tongue, then flew away, following the witch toward the Witches Cemetery. Mikael and I shook hands, and he promised me that if I wanted it, he would help me escape next. We agreed to work together, to free both of us from slavery.

"If you're ever in need of help, you have only to call on me," He said in his monotonous Scandinavian voice. "I am in your debt."

He'd already helped me by slipping me the note about Harry. I never would have known about the death if it hadn't been for Mikael. But now he was doing something even more vital – finding another witch who could perform the same rite on me.

Now he was in danger. I had to get to him before Sir Thomas' servants did.

I flew over the wall surrounding the Carnarvon property, my path crooked as the ring tightened around my wing. The pain was getting worse. I resisted the urge to peck at the ring, to try to dislodge it. I knew from years of trying that was fruitless. *I just need to hold on a little longer ...*

The Bran roost was toward the rear of the garden. If Mikael wasn't on patrol he would be there. As I dipped lower, I noticed several cars and a white van parked in the drive. The cars flashed their lights. People rushed in all directions. *The police are here, and an ambulance ...*

I swooped lower, a sinking feeling settling on me as I registered the scene below. Several black feathers littered the front steps of the hall. Two ambulance officers wheeled a body covered with a sheet across the lawn. I didn't have to get any closer to figure out who it was.

Shit.

My warning would come too late for Mikael.

15

BELINDA

I didn't want to involve the police. I was worried alerting the authorities might somehow come back to bite Cole, but Ryan insisted. "You never know when it could come in handy to have this crime on record," he said. So I called my old friend Detective Sanders, who had been the officer in charge of Ethan's case. I still knew his number by heart. He came around with the faithful Sergeant MacAllister, who busied himself immediately taking photographs of the mess.

"I'll get the SOC unit over to have a look as soon as I can," Detective Sanders explained as he scribbled down notes. "They're currently out at Crooks Crossing, at the scene of a particularly gruesome murder."

"That's fine." Talking to Sanders gave me a terrible feeling of deja vu. Every time I tried to speak, my words would catch on the lump in my throat. I was trying desperately to keep my tears at bay, but standing in the entrance looking at the mess was testing the limits of my composure.

"In the meantime, please don't touch or move anything. As soon as the SOCOs are done, you can start to clean up." Sanders cleared his throat. "I have to ask, have you seen him around lately? Has he tried to contact you?"

"I ... I don't know." I whispered, hugging my arms to myself. "I thought I saw him on the street the other night, just leaning up against that crystal shop across the road. But I didn't get a good look at him. It could have been anyone."

"Oh, Belinda." Alex squeezed my hand. "You should have said something."

Sanders scribbled that down. "And you can't think of anyone else who might have reason to do this?"

Oh, just a couple of homicidal ravens employed by the richest family in the county, and some guy named Gillespie who I'm not supposed to talk about. "I don't know anyone else who ... who hates me ... so much."

It was too much, too much. The lump in my throat grew larger. I turned away from the shop, blinking away a stray tear that trickled down my cheek.

"Don't worry," Detective Sanders looked me in the eyes. "I haven't given up. We will get him, Belinda. Guys like Ethan are too smug, too pleased with their own genius. Sooner or later, they get cocky. They slip up, and we'll be ready to swoop in."

"Sure," I croaked. Sanders asked me a couple more questions, and I answered as best I could, my mind working on autopilot. I watched MacCallister pawing through the remains of my broken kitchen.

"Have you called your insurance company?" MacCallister called out. "They're going to want to see this."

"I don't have insurance." I mumbled. I'd had to stop paying the premiums, so I could afford flour for the bread. The tears in my eyes spilled over again. *How am I going to repair all this? I'll have to close. I'll have to sell everything. But then how will I pay the debt ...*

I felt a reassuring hand slide around my shoulder. "Come on." Alex led me away. "Let's go to the pub."

The pub. Yes, that was what I needed. A stiff drink.

My legs were shaking so hard that I wasn't certain I'd even make it to *Tir Na Nog*, but as soon as I sank down into the bar stool, I knew I'd come to the right place.

"Get me a gin and tonic," I told Ryan. "And make it light on the tonic. In fact, I'll have two."

"One for me as well," Alex said, placing her arm around me. Ryan wandered off to the bar.

I placed my head in my hands, tears streaming down my cheeks. They came thick and fast now, all that held-in emotion welling out of me and streaming down my face. My chest felt tight, and there were pins and needles stabbing at my heart. I kept thinking about my overdrawn bank account and my huge credit card debt and my lack of insurance and the fact that I couldn't open the shop again until all the mess was cleaned up. I was going to lose weeks of business, not to mention all those supplies, all the tables and decorations I'd lovingly chosen. The task of digging myself out of this mess seemed impossible.

Gone, all gone. Finally, Ethan had taken everything from me.

"Belinda, I'm so sorry." Alex patted my back. She had that tone in her voice where she was trying to be reassuring, but didn't know what to say. I couldn't blame her. There was nothing positive about this, no lemonade to be made. I tried to say something to her, to tell her it was okay, but I couldn't even form words. All that came out was a strangled sob.

"Oh, girl. It will be all right. You'll see. We'll find who did this, and Cole and Ryan will make them pay. We'll all help you do the repairs – Ryan and Elinor and Bianca and I, we'll all pitch in – and *Bewitching Bites* will be up and running again before you know it."

I shook my head, burying my face into my hands. Everything seemed hopeless. I couldn't see a way to fix this. I would have to sell the shop. I would have to go back to my mother's house and live in my old room and listen to her smug husband go on and on about how he'd *told* me retail was a loser's game—

Alex was glancing all around the restaurant. "That's odd," she said.

"What's odd?" I glanced up briefly from my misery, but didn't notice anything out of the ordinary.

"Well, there seem to be quite a lot of people in here for a Thursday morning, and they're all staring at the TV, but there's no footy game on. It's only the local news station talking about a murder. And both of the waitresses are crying."

"Huh?" I couldn't even bring myself to care. So what if everyone in the pub was acting weird? At least they all had homes and businesses to go back to. At least they had lives. I had *nothing.*

"Can I get you ladies anything?" A sniffly voice interrupted my thoughts. The waitress had come over. She dabbed a napkin in the corners of her eyes, not even noticing that I was drowning in my own sorrow. I took a longer look at the waitress' swollen eyes and blotchy face. She didn't look much better off than me.

"We could do with a beef and Guinness pie to go with our drinks, and a slice of peanut butter cheesecake to shar," Alex said. She reached over and touched the girl's arm. "What's going on, honey? Are you okay? You look really upset."

"Didn't you hear?" The waitress wiped another stream of tears from her face. "Mikael's dead. He's been murdered."

I snapped my head up. Mikael – the Bran bartender who'd given Cole the note and driven us the other night – was dead? "Murdered?"

"Yeah, apparently someone snuck onto the estate he lives on out in Crooks Crossing. They got him while he slept, so he didn't stand a chance. Rachel went over to look for him after he didn't show up this morning, she found the body. They ..." she sobbed. "They tortured him. His whole body was covered in tiny cuts. The police say he slowly bled to death. He was missing two pints of blood. It's just ... I can't believe ..."

She walked away, still sobbing. Alex turned back to me. "Wow, that's rough. I don't think we'll be getting our pies."

I nodded, too stunned to say anything. First my shop was destroyed, and then Mikael shows up dead. There was no way this was a coincidence. It could only mean one thing.

Cole was being followed. Someone knew that he was alive, and they were pissed as hell.

~

I FIGURED we were safe enough in the pub, in broad daylight, surrounded by people. We polished off another two rounds before we eventually got our food. I checked my phone and found four messages from Elinor, who had come round to the shop at her usual time and seen the police tape. I tapped out a reply, then put my phone away. I couldn't bear to think about it anymore. Just telling Elinor made my chest ache with sadness.

Ryan declared that I would need to come and stay with them at Raynard Hall. "We have strong protective charms there," he said. "If there's anyone else Cole has talked to who you think might be in danger, we should bring them in, also. I don't want to see anyone else dead."

I thought back over my interactions with Cole. "Just his brother, Byron. But I still can't figure out if he's a friend or enemy. And Chairman Meow, of course. And maybe my friend Elinor, just to be safe. She's talked to Cole a couple of times."

Alex's eyes lit up. "Yeah, let's get Elinor over. We can even ask Bianca, too. It will be like a sleepover."

The thought lifted my spirits a little. It was rare that I got to see all my girlfriends altogether outside of the shop. At Ryan's house we'd be safe, and maybe they could take my mind off the shop and help me figure out my feelings for Cole. "It's a great idea. Let's visit the shop on the way back and ask. Ryan, has Simon set that meeting with Thomas Gillespie yet?"

Ryan shook his head. "He texted me to say he'd called their hotel in Northampton, but they told him the Gillespies checked out yesterday. I'm concerned they could already be in Loamshire. When we get home I'll look up some of my local contacts and see if I can find them. I hope Cole has been sensible enough to lay low today."

Knowing Cole, probably not. "We should go back to the hall," I said, suddenly desperate to see Cole, to feel his arms around me, his kisses on my lips. It seemed like the only thing that could cure the sadness that threatened to overwhelm me. "It's not as if I can do anything more in the shop today."

We went back to the shop, and the destruction greeted me at the door, reminding me again just how unfair this was. I slumped into one of the few unbroken chairs, too exhausted to consider going back up to my apartment.

"We could start cleaning up." Alex offered. "Maybe get some of the tables repaired—"

I shook my head. "That's kind, but no. I can't deal with it right now. Tomorrow maybe. I just ... need some time to process it, figure out what to do next. Plus, we should go get Elinor and Bianca."

"You're right. I'll go pack some stuff for you," Alex started upstairs.

"No!" I cried out, rising from my chair. Somehow, I'd managed to avoid letting the others see the flat all day. If Alex went up there now, she'd see the sparseness of it, and she'd *know.* She'd know I was a failure. "I'll do it. I know where everything is."

"Nonsense," Ryan placed a hand on my shoulder and pushed me back down. "Stay right here. Detective Sanders said there's a bit of damage up there, too. You don't need any more frights right now."

"But—"

"No buts." Alex slipped through my fingers and bounded up the stairs before I could stop her.

I sat back, miserable and helpless, a lead weight in my chest as Alex clumped around upstairs. She returned fifteen minutes later with a tote bag full of clothes and toiletries, and a cardboard box containing a howling Chairman Meow. "I think that's everything," she said.

"Thank you," I mumbled, knowing from her penetrating look that she was going to grill me about the flat later. Now that was something to look forward to.

"Great. Let's go." Ryan ushered us into the car. I took one last lingering look at my bakery as we sped away, the police tape around the entrance flapping in the wind. The lead in my stomach sank deeper. I felt as though I were leaving it behind forever.

16

COLE

*A*fter watching Mikael's lifeless body being wheeled into the morgue, I dared a journey back to the Crooks Crossing churchyard. Of course, Gillespie and his servants were no longer there. The lid of the sarcophagus had been replaced, and the tomb thoroughly cleaned, as though they had never been there at all. I had no idea where Sir Thomas was hiding now, but I knew it would not be long now until he went to visit Morchard. If he found Byron, I'd be dead, and so would Belinda.

I was returning to Raynard Hall just as Alex's car was pulling up the drive. Odd. They shouldn't be coming back from the bakery yet. And they had two other passengers in the backseat – the curvy Elinor who I'd seen in the bakery talking to Belinda, and another girl with bright blue hair. I flew down from the eaves and settled on the front step, tapping the ground with my beak to get them to hurry up.

Belinda stepped out of the car, her head hung low. Her eyes were red, and her skin puffy. She'd been crying. *What happened? Is she hurt?*

I forced a shift. A few seconds later I was sitting naked on the step, in my human form. I started to get up to go to Belinda, but Ryan held up his hand to stop me.

"Just because she doesn't mind your naked body doesn't mean I have to be subjected to it." Ryan moved to the back of the car and lifted the boot.

"I have to see Belinda." I growled, striding toward him.

"Oh, don't let me stop you." Alex licked her lips.

"Or me," said Elinor.

"My house, my rules." Ryan tossed me a pair of shorts, which I obligingly pulled on. Elinor and the blue-haired girl made pouting faces at each other. As I walked around the car to Belinda, I peered into the boot. "You have a whole wardrobe in here? Are you on *Project Runway*?"

Ryan laughed. "No, I just like to keep spares on hand in case I need to shift in a pinch. I even have clothes stashed around the village and all through the forest, in case I'm caught somewhere."

"Clever." It didn't surprise me – vulpines were always clever. Belinda looked up at me, forcing a smile. I took one look at her stricken face and ran to her, throwing my arms around her as she collapsed against me, her whole body sagging. "What happened?"

"The bakery," she sniffed, burying her head in my shoulder. "It's destroyed."

"What?"

"It's true," Alex said. Briefly she explained what they'd seen when they opened the bakery, and what the police had said. Belinda buried herself deeper into my shoulder, her whole body racked with silent sobs.

I helped her up the steps to the door, my blood boiling with rage. Belinda looked so deflated, like a balloon that had been pierced with a pin. She was exactly the opposite from the way she looked last night. I gritted my teeth as I waited for Ryan's butler to arrive at the door. I needed to get Belinda alone so I could assure her that whoever did this was going to have his throat ripped out.

"That bakery was my life," she choked between sobs. "It was the only thing that was keeping me going, and now it's gone."

This is all your fault. My mind nagged at me. A wave of guilt eradicated the rage in my blood. *If you hadn't got her involved in this, then she would still have her business, and her life.*

"I'll get the person who did this to you," I said, picturing the smirking face of Victor Morchard crumpling as I pounded it to a pulp. The image made me feel slightly better about the guilt tugging at my heart.

"He hates me this much," she sobbed. "That's the only reason he would do this."

"Who would do this?"

"Ethan."

"I don't think your ex did this," I told her, rubbing her shoulders.

"Of course he did. He wants to take everything from me. You don't understand how he thinks, but I do. I deserve this. I'm such an awful person, that's why he hates me. It's all my fault."

What? Is she serious?

"No, hush." I pulled her hands from her eyes. "Look at me. You can't talk like that. You are the exact opposite of an awful person. You are wonderful, and kind, and incredibly beautiful. And hot as fuck."

She scoffed. "Whatever. If I'm so kind and beautiful and wonderful, then why did he leave me? Why did he take everything from me?"

The words stung, the fact she was still thinking about him, still caring what *he* thought. That thieving bastard had really done a number on Belinda's psyche. I gripped her chin between my fingers, pulling her face up so she could see my face. She kept her eyes cast downward. The rivers of tears streaming down her cheeks turned my blood hot with anger, burning through the pain that tried to pull me back to my master. The idea that

Belinda thought so little of herself hurt more than all the pain Victor Morchard could inflict.

"You want to know why? Because he's an arsehole, and he's lucky I haven't caught up with him yet, because I would stick my boot so far up his arse people will think Doc Martens have started making hats. Don't for a second let that dickshit dictate how you feel about yourself. You are an *amazing* person, Belinda. You rescued a bird in danger, you took in a man who needed a place to crash, you treated me with dignity and respect even though I'm no more than a slave. You battled through all your troubles with extreme resilience, you even put up with that idiotic kid out of some kind of grim obligation. But you don't have to do it on your own anymore. I'm not going to let you. As soon as you and I are both safe, we are going to get your store back, and we are going to do something about those debts. You deserve your life back, Belinda. And I promise you I will do everything in my power to ensure you get it."

She looked up at me then, her eyes such intense orbs of despair, that I had to do something to bring her back from the brink of darkness. I wasn't very good at saying the right thing, but I knew one thing I could do.

I pressed my lips to hers, and prised her mouth open, thrusting my tongue inside. I poured all of my passion for her into the kiss, trying to show her how I felt about her.

Slowly, the tension in Belinda's body slipped away, and she kissed me back with ferocious intensity. She wrapped her arms around me, burying her fingers in my hair, a little mewling noise emitting from the back of her throat.

Behind me, I could hear the other girls clapping and whistling. As much as I liked an audience, I didn't think they'd want to see what I was about to do to Belinda. I picked Belinda up and carried her unsteadily through the labyrinth of halls to our rooms, my mouth never leaving hers and my hardon slapping impatiently against my thigh the entire way. My leg twinged with every step, and the ring pulsed angrily, but I was getting good at ignoring them both, especially when she was in my arms.

I kicked open the door to Belinda's room, and manoeuvred her inside. I tossed her on the bed. She bounced a little on the soft mattress. I leaned over her, loving the way her hair fanned out around her delicate face, and smothered her with kisses. She wrapped her legs around my body, pulling me against her, grinding her pelvis against my engorged cock. Christ, that was hot. I tore off her shirt, revealing her beautiful body. She kicked off her own shorts, and leaned back against the covers, begging me with her eyes to follow.

I pulled off my own clothes and slipped on a condom. It took only moments to remove Belinda's bra and panties, and then I was looking down at that stunning woman in all her naked beauty once more.

I could see in Belinda's eyes that this wasn't the time to be tender. She didn't want the space to think about what was happening. She just wanted to *be*. That I could provide for her. I flipped her over on her front and pushed her legs apart with my knee. I grabbed her thighs and pulled her back, impaling her on my cock with one powerful thrust.

"Oh, Cole!" she cried out, tossing her head back as I plowed into her. She gripped the bedsheets and pushed her hips back against me, grinding herself against my cock with incredible force. I loved this view, kneeling on the bed and looking down at her writhing body, her black hair tossing wildly across her silken back as she pushed back against each thrust.

I leaned over her, steadying my body with one hand while I thrust the other beneath her. I took her nipple between my fingers and twisted it. She cried out, biting into my arm and growling between her teeth.

"Too hard?" I whispered in her ear, concerned I had hurt her.

"No, I want more. Harder!" Belinda cried, her shoulders tensing as she slammed her pelvis back against mine. *If you insist.*

I twisted the other nipple. Belinda ground back against me, tossing her head back, and presenting me with her bare neck. I bit down on her shoulder as I continued to twist her nipple, and she growled again.

"You like it hard?" I growled in her ear.

"I love it!" she moaned back, her walls tightening around my cock as her body responded. "More!"

I was right about Belinda. She had a hidden dirty girl side, and now, that girl had come out to play.

Belinda bucked against me, her moans growing louder, more urgent. I reached around further and touched my fingers to her clit. "Yes, Cole, yes!" she cried, grinding against me as I stimulated her. Her orgasm came quickly, her whole body shuddering as her walls contracted around me, squeezing me inside her. The sensation was so hot I almost sent myself over the edge. I stopped thrusting for a moment, taking a few deep breaths before I continued.

I liked this girl. I liked her a *lot*.

Even though she'd just come, Belinda continued to grind herself against my cock, pushing me as deep as I could go. I sat up again and gripped her thighs, stroking her shapely ass as I watched myself thrust inside her.

I stroked my fingers over her skin, then lightly slapped each cheek, loving the sound my hand made as it connected with her flesh. Belinda gasped with pleasure, encouraging me to explore her further. I pushed my fingers against her sex, coating them with her juices, then ran them along her crack, pulling apart her cheeks and stroking the edge of her back hole, gently, slowly. I didn't know if she was into this.

"Yes!" she screamed.

I guess she is into this. Grinning, I slipped one finger inside. Belinda gasped again, and rammed herself against me so hard I nearly fell off the bed. I leaned forward slightly, pushing my other hand beneath her, finding her clit. I stoked her with one hand as I pushed my other finger deeper inside her. I couldn't keep my thrusts as powerful, but she ground back against me, pleasuring herself as I stimulated her from all sides. In a few minutes, she was coming again, her screams loud enough to shake the windows.

This girl. I couldn't get enough of her.

Dirty Belinda was not done yet. She leaned her head against the bed and shoved her hands between our legs. At first I thought she was stimulating herself, but she ran her fingers over my balls, pulling them slightly, causing a little tenderness that only fuelled my desire. I pulled my finger from her and grabbed her thighs again, guiding her in a steady rhythm. She leaned back further and used one finger to stroke the sensitive skin that stretched between my balls and arse. Every time I pulled out and thrust into her, she would stroke that skin.

My own orgasm built quickly, the heat emanating out from my core. I wasn't going to be able to hold on much longer.

"You should stop doing that," I growled in her ear. "If you want this to last longer. I'm so close right now."

In response, she dragged her nail across that skin again.

"*Ooooooh fuck!*" I cried out as I came hard, harder than I ever had before. My body spasmed against hers, my fingers digging into her thighs as I held her still so I could pump into her. Belinda cried out as a final orgasm hit her at the same time.

I saw stars. Bright lights swam in front of my eyes. My head spun, the room disappeared. The pain in my body faded away. I lost all sense of why I was or where I was. All that existed was the pleasure that coursed through my body, an intense heat that almost burned me up, it was so powerful.

Wow. I had never come like *that* before.

As the fire in my body started to fade, and the lights in my eyes disappeared, I collapsed against the bed, utterly spent. The pain crept back, coursing through my veins and poisoning the beauty of the moment. I pulled Belinda against my body, wrapping my arms around her. I wanted to be as close to her as I could get. I kissed a line down the side of her cheek, breathing in the exquisite smell of her.

"Thank you, Cole." She gripped my arm with her hands, her eyes fluttering closed. "I needed that."

"You're welcome," I whispered in her ear. As I cuddled with her, running my hands over her gorgeous skin, I realised that this hadn't been a selfless act, not really. I wanted to make her feel better, to forget her pain for a while. But more than that, I was trying to drive out my guilt with my cock. And I hadn't succeeded. I may have satisfied her, but I hadn't got her shop back. I hadn't made her life any more safe. In all aspects except one, I was coming up short. I'd done nothing to show I was worthy of her.

Belinda was a beautiful angel, and I was the worst kind of bastard.

17

BELINDA

*B*y the time we emerged from the bedroom, Elinor and Bianca were already lounging comfortably in one of the drawing rooms, a bottle of wine lying empty between them. Two sleeping cats taking up the rug in front of the fire. The girls clapped as we entered the room, and I turned a deep shade of red.

"I see the Chairman has made a new friend already." I knelt down beside the cats and stroked them both. Chairman raised his head as if to say, "I could get used to this," then flopped back down in front of the fire.

Alex set Elinor and Bianca up with rooms in the same wing as mine. Cole pointed out in his tactful way that they should take the rooms on the end of the hallway, as far from ours as possible. Elinor gave me an amused look and I turned even more horrifically crimson.

Having my girlfriends in the house was great. They distracted me from the overwhelming sadness at losing my shop. Alex and Bianca took over Ryan's designer kitchen and made a batch of rocky road slice. Despite my being the baking expert, they refused to let me help. Instead, Elinor and I opened another bottle of wine, painted each other's nails and giggled our way through the latest Hugh Grant film on Ryan's enormous TV. Chairman Meow – bored of the fire now – spent fifteen minutes cautiously sniffing his way around the drawing room, and then curled up inside the liquor cabinet. Cole and Ryan retreated to the study where they could talk about shifter things.

Eventually, Simon kicked the girls out of the kitchen so he could make the dinner. We sat down to a beautiful meal of herb-crusted salmon and lemon-roasted vegetables. After dinner Elinor curled up in the study with her phone to talk to Eric – who was recording the new Ghost Symphony album at a studio in London – while everyone else poured wine and played some kind of rude card game that was all the rage. The Chairman claimed a large velvet chair in the corner, and Miss Havisham sat regally atop the back of Alex's chair, as though it were a throne – they both spent the remainder of the evening casting judgement upon all of us, as only cats can do.

"Do you want to go for a walk?" Cole asked hopefully as I finished my sixth glass of wine. "Things have become a little crowded in here. I'd like to talk to you alone."

I rubbed my eyes, suddenly overcome with weariness. I really had to get some sleep, but I couldn't say no to Cole. At least I didn't have to get up at 3:30 the next morning—

No. I didn't want to think about it. If I started worrying about the bakery, I'd never get any sleep. *Cole.* He was a good distraction.

"Sure," I said.

We wandered out the French doors to the gardens. Ryan followed us, slumping into one of the deck chairs with a glass of Scotch in his hand. "Don't mind me, I like to come out and enjoy the moonlight."

"We won't," Cole growled, bending down to kiss me roughly. My heart clenched as I bent up to return the kiss. How was it he managed to make me forget my problems so completely?

"Come on," Cole grabbed my hand and pulled me down the steps at the end of the patio. I jogged after him between the flowerbeds as we moved toward the large stone fountain in the middle of the round pool that formed the focal point of the garden.

"Don't go too far," Ryan called after us. "You're being watched."

I whirled around, my heart leaping in my chest as I searched for some sinister looking villain. "I thought this place was protected by charms."

Ryan grinned. "It is." He pointed up at the stone statue of the goddess Diana that fed the fountain. I could just make out the silhouette of a dark shape perched on the statue's shoulder.

The bird turned to us, and let out a menacing "croak."

I cried out and leapt back. Cole grabbed me, his strong arms wrapping tight around me. His breath was hot against my ear. "Don't worry. It's only Byron. Ryan has allowed him to enter the protected area of the house. He's making good on his promise to watch out for me."

I relaxed a little. "He's a good brother, then."

"If you say so." Cole glared at the bird as we walked around the edge of the fountain, heading toward the darkened forest.

"What is this animosity between the two of you?"

Cole sighed. "Do you really want to know?"

"Of course I do. I want to understand."

"Byron is the older of us, by five years. He's always resented me running around after him. To him, I was just this annoying kid who ruined all his fun. It got worse after my father died, and as my mother got sicker and sicker. He just didn't want to be around us, so he would go off with Pax and Poe, and I would be stuck keeping her company." He saw my face. "Don't get me wrong, I didn't mind staying with my mother. I loved her dearly. She was such a genuinely kind person. You remind me of her."

"I hope that's a compliment." I beamed.

"It is the highest compliment. Anyway, after a couple of years, my mother's illness got so bad she couldn't work any longer. She wasn't able to shift to her human form, and her bones started to fuse together. She couldn't unfurl her wings or bend her neck. It was awful to watch."

"Oh, Cole. I'm so sorry."

"Yeah," he stared off into the distance. "I'm sorry, too. Morchard, of course, couldn't bear to have a Bran that wasn't performing, so he took her into his aviary. At first, he kept up a pretense he was trying to cure her, and I believed him, because I was a fool. I visited her every day when I could get away from my duties, and despite all the drugs Morchard gave her, she got worse and worse. It was so bad she could hardly speak. She couldn't move. She was trapped inside her own skin."

To watch someone you loved go through that ... it must have been awful. I squeezed Cole's hand, tears forming in the edges of my eyes.

"I believe now that Morchard was deliberately keeping her sick and immobile, so he could extract samples from her and experiment while she was still alive. But, of course, I have no proof of that. I thought he was helping her." He spat bitterly. "One afternoon, he summoned me and Byron to his laboratory. I came right away, but Byron didn't. He was off with Pax and Poe. Morchard said she was dying. I sat with her for hours, stroking her and waiting for the end, waiting for Byron to show up to say goodbye. But he never did."

"Shit." That explained a lot. Byron was the older brother. He was supposed to protect Cole from that kind of pain. But he had deserted Cole when he needed him most, and Cole couldn't forgive him. I suspected Byron probably hadn't forgiven himself.

"Yeah."

A cold silence descended between us. I searched for something else to say, but couldn't think.

"Please, don't think of it anymore," Cole said. "Don't let Byron destroy our evening."

"Oh, no. I wouldn't dare."

When we were clear of the raised beds and topiaries, Cole grabbed my hand. A warm jolt flicked up my arm. I turned to him and gave a small smile.

"This is nice," I said. What I really meant was, *kiss me*. I wet my lips, gazing up at him expectantly.

But if Cole understood the message, he didn't act on it. He stared down at his feet. "I'm so sorry about your bakery."

I didn't want to think about it now, out here with him. "It's okay. It's not your fault."

"Did you really see your ex across the street the other night? I wish you had said something."

"I don't know what I saw. That's exactly why I didn't mention it. It *can't* be Ethan. He wouldn't be so stupid as to show up here and do this. At least, I wouldn't have thought so. It's not his style. It's a bit ... sloppy."

"That's what I was afraid of." Cole rubbed the line of stubble along his chin. "And that black feather you found was clearly a message. The only thing I can't figure out is who is it a message from. Is it Thomas Gillespie, telling me that he knows where you are, and if I don't submit to him, he'll hurt you? Or is it Morchard, telling you that he knows you've been hiding me? Or is it someone else with some skin in this game who hasn't made their presence known yet?"

The same questions had been running around my head all afternoon, but I was no closer to solving them. "I don't want to think about it right now. We're safe here, for now. Ryan will try to locate Gillespie in the morning. Maybe we can sort this all out without any more violence."

"I highly doubt that." Cole squeezed my hand extra tight. "I just want to keep you safe."

"I'm safe here with you. Now, please. Can we talk about something else?" The night air blew a cool breeze across my skin. I laced my fingers into Cole's. He ran his thumb over my knuckles, and I loved the way that simple touch made my heart skip.

"Very well. What made you want to open a bakery?"

Now that one I could answer. "When I was a kid, my dad travelled a lot for work. He's white, born in Surrey. He was an executive at a cell phone company, so we were quite well-off. My mother was his PA." Cole gave me an amused look. I shrugged. "You're right. It's exactly what it sounds like. She was twelve years his junior. She'd arrived in England from China with nothing but the clothes on her back and the determination to work hard and find herself a husband to look after her. It was quite the office scandal when their affair became public, but they were madly in love. After they got married, mum decided to give up her career and stay home to manage the house and look after me. Lots of the other executive kids had nannies, but not me. I had mum. She didn't miss the office at all. She even home-schooled me for a time, and she was always coming up with fantastic outings and games for me.

"Before she married Dad, she'd never even boiled an egg before, but she got really interested in cooking. We used to spend the day together knocking up scones and cakes. She taught me Chinese recipes her mother used to make for her, but we both preferred the heavy, hearty English food and baking. Dad would take the leftovers into work and tell everyone proudly what his daughter had created. I loved spending that time with my mum, and I loved the way fresh-baked bread and pies smelled, and I loved it that my dad was so proud of what I'd done, I guess."

"Your parents sound wonderful."

"Do they?" My head snapped up. I'd been lost in the memory. I'd almost forgotten he was there. "I suppose they were, at least in the beginning. But it didn't last. When I was ten, my dad got ousted during a company restructure, and he struggled to find another job. My mum had to go back to work, so that was the end of the home cooking. We were a takeout and nanny family, just like everyone else. My parents were always tired and always fighting, mostly about money. I think my mum resented my dad for losing his job and forcing her back to work, and my dad resented mum for making him feel bad.

"Our house was such a toxic place to be. I couldn't stand it. I had to do something to try to get it back to the way things were. So I took over in the kitchen. I started doing all the cooking. I packed them both lunches every day. After a while my mum just handed me the grocery money each month. I saved them a lot of money on crappy takeout, but I couldn't save their marriage."

"Oh, Belinda. I'm so sorry."

"I don't really want to talk about it," I said, tears brimming in the corners of my eyes. Great, I was crying about everything today.

"It's good to talk. It gets the blood flowing for all the other things we're going to get up to tonight." Cole brushed his lips across mine, sending a shiver of desire through my body. "What happened next?"

"They divorced when I was fifteen. Dad stayed in London, and mom moved us to Crookshollow, where her mother now lived. I finished up school here, went to culinary school in London, came back, met Ethan, opened the shop, got my heart ripped out. Mum met Gary," I made a face. "He's twenty-six years older than her. She got botox. They moved to Liverpool and live in one of those houses that looks like it belongs on *Footballers Wives*. She hired a cook and got one of those little yappy dogs. I don't really see her that much."

"You sound disappointed in her."

I shrugged. "I guess. I just ... she's so different now. I guess I wonder if this was how she always was, and her old playfulness was a show for my benefit. Dad's no different. He started his own company, doing telecom for corporate clients. He has a string of young, leggy blonde girlfriends."

"Can I ask a really personal question?" Cole squeezed my hand again, placing his other hand on top of my fingers.

"I might not answer." It was hard to stay guarded when he touched me like that.

"When Ethan took all your stuff, why didn't you go to your parents for help? They both sound as though they're relatively well-off. I'm sure they'd be happy to help you—"

I shook my head so vigorously I wrenched my neck. I winced. "No. I have to do this myself."

"Why?"

"Because. I just do. Can we please change the subject?" I noticed he was leaning heavily on one leg. The leg that hadn't been injured. "I haven't asked you how your leg is doing today. Is it feeling better?"

"It's fine."

"You sound so sincere."

Cole showed me his finger. It looked tiny compared to his other fingers, and the skin had shriveled up, and was turning black. I held my hand near the glowing ring, feeling the heat rise from that mysterious metal surface. I sucked in my breath, unable to understand how he was standing upright still. The pain must be excruciating.

"I hardly even think about my leg," Cole said. "With this on my finger, sending stabbing pain through my body every few moments."

"How do you stand it?"

"I have to, so I do." Cole pulled his hand away. "It is a small price to pay to be with you."

Tears sprang in my eyes at the thought of him enduring this for me. "Cole, we have to do something. You'll lose your finger."

"Nightingale, it's okay." He held my arm with his good hand. "You don't have to worry about me. I'm here to look after *you*."

"That's easy for you to say. You're not the one who heard that poor, hurt raven crying for help, or it's pathetic whining when I cleaned its wound."

"I didn't whine, and I can fly just fine."

"Oh yeah?" I grinned. "Then let me see you fly."

Cole stepped away from me, and jumped up on the edge of the fountain, his body moving like a graceful dancer. He turned to me, planting his weight on his good leg, and started to shift.

Cole's body shrunk down into itself, his arms pulling back into the sleeves of his shirt, his legs crumpling beneath him. His nose grew out from his face, becoming long and hooked and hard, while his chin reached up to meet it. From his skin sprouted the dark bristles, which fanned out and became jet feathers, folding over themselves in a graceful pattern. His whole body seemed to disappear into the darkened forest beyond.

"You look ridiculous," I told him, grinning again. In reality, I found his shift fascinating, and kind of a turn-on. It was amazing to think that a body could perform such a remarkable feat. I would think it some kind of magic, and I guess in a way it was. But it wasn't the kind of magic I saw on TV shows, with smoke and explosions. This was something much more ancient, much more primal. And it was part of Cole.

From his elbows extended long bones that grew more skin and bristles, and these great black feathers that became his beautiful wings. As Cole shrank down, he disappeared inside of his clothes, which crumpled into a pile on the edge of the fountain.

For a few moments, there was complete silence, and then the lump inside the clothes moved, and I heard a faint *squawk*.

"Oh, you're all tangled up." I reached over to lift off the shirt. With a much louder squawk, Cole bounced out from beneath his clothes, flapped his wings, and took to the air. He swooped and dived, performing elaborate rolls and flips in the air, his streamlined body appearing more like a plane than a bird.

"OK, I get the idea!" I laughed. "You can change back now. You're clearly just fine."

Cole zoomed past at high speed. I nodded in appreciation, watching him hurtle his body toward the dark trees.

Suddenly, another black blur emerged from the forest and crashed into him, knocking him from the sky. "Cole!" I yelled, running across the lawn toward them. In the darkness I couldn't see what was happening, but I heard Cole's frantic screech. Behind me, I heard footsteps pound across the cobbles as Ryan tore towards us.

The only reply I heard was a loud squawk, cut abruptly short by a high-pitched, inhuman screech.

It was Byron. It had to be. That bastard had sweet-talked Cole into getting him behind the protective spells, and then attacked him when his guard was down. *I knew it. I'd had such a bad feeling about him, and now he's hurting Cole. Where are they?*

"Cole!" I cried out, darting across the lawn. I scanned the ground in front of me. Where were they? The screeching grew louder, but it seemed to have more than one voice. It came from all around me.

Then I heard the flapping.

My heart pounded against my chest. I whirled around, searching the forest for the source of the sound. The screeching grew louder. I saw what at first appeared to be a black cloud rising over the tops of the trees. As the whirring, flapping noise grew louder I realised to my horror that was no cloud, it was a massive flock of ravens. Hundreds of them descended upon Ryan's garden, their dark, beady eyes trained on me.

As one unit, they launched themselves at me. I turned and ran toward the house. I could just make out the shape of Ryan, now in his fox form, as he launched himself across the lawn. I tried to yell at him to get to Cole, but my words were lost as the black cloud swirled around me.

The birds flew so close together that they completely blocked out my view of the house. I stumbled forward, completely blind, my arms stretched out in front of me. *Where's the steps? Where's the edge of the fountain?* All I could feel as I moved slowly across the lawn was the beating of their wings against my skin.

"Cole!" I cried out, helpless as the birds swarmed around me, their wings slicing over my skin, their claws digging into my clothing. My shirt tore, and tears sprang to my eyes. *Where's Cole? What's happening? What are they doing to me?* I pictured myself pecked to death, covered with tiny wounds like poor Mikael. I stumbled forward in the darkness, flailing my hands around, trying to beat them off, but the birds only tightened their circle,

"What's happening?"

Panic seized me as my feet left the ground, and soon I was dangling in the air above the graves, my vision a blur of black feathers and cruel, beady eyes. I opened my mouth to scream, only to find myself choking on feathers. The ravens dragged me higher still... calling to each other with excited croaks as they carried me off.

Their bodies pressed tighter against me, and everything went black.

TO BE CONTINUED

∿

Cole and Belinda's story concludes in book 6 of the Crookshollow Gothic Romance series, *Reaper*. Read Reaper now!

∿

Want free books, exclusive giveaways and exclusive sneak peeks at upcoming Steffanie Holmes paranormal romance books? Sign up at www.steffanieholmes.com to get the scoop.

EXCERPT FROM REAPER

CROOKSHOLLOW GOTHIC ROMANCE, BOOK 6

I bolted upright, my hand reaching for my heart. I gasped for air, my chest heavy, as though something had been crushing it. I blinked, my eyes adjusting to the gloom. Light streamed in the window from the moon outside, but there was no ethereal white light coming from the hallway. There was no beautiful man in my bed. I was all alone.

I touched my lips, still feeling the warmth of his mouth lingering there.

It was just a dream. But it had felt so *real*. My body still tingled where Cole had touched me. My sex clenched from his presence. My core throbbed with the remnants of my orgasm.

Cole had been *here*. I'd felt him. But how? He didn't have the power to do that kind of thing, did he? That was some kind of ... astral projection? It couldn't be. Cole was still tethered to Libby, he couldn't use that kind of power to do something like this without her willing him.

Knowing I would never be able to go back to sleep, I turned on the bedside lamp. Two black feathers rested on the duvet in front of me.

Cole.

I picked them up and cradled them in my hand, tears of joy streaming down my face. I don't know how he'd done it, but he was giving me a sign. He was telling me he would come back for me. He was mine.

He loved me. Cole *loved* me. And that love could give me the strength I needed to do what I had to do.

～

Want to find out more? READ REAPER NOW

EXCERPT FROM DIGGING THE WOLF

Luke whirled around, the light of his torch temporarily blinding me. "Anna, you startled me."

"I might say the same thing," I said, suddenly nervous. It had been curiosity that compelled me to follow him into the caves, to see why he was sneaking around the site at night after explicitly warning us not to. But now that I was here, confronting him wearing only my pyjamas, thermal underwear, boots, and jacket, I realised just how dangerous this situation could be. I barely knew Luke. Just because he was gorgeous didn't mean he didn't have some nefarious purpose. As far as I knew, the guy could be unstable. And I was alone with him, without my hard hat, in the dark, in an unexplored section of the cave. No one else knew I was here. If he killed me now, they wouldn't ever find my body.

I'd just made all the mistakes I'd promised myself I'd never make.

"I asked a question," I said, trying to stop my voice from wavering. Luke stared at me with wide eyes. His mouth moved, but no sound came out. Fancy that. I'd actually rendered him speechless.

"Luke?" I prodded, careful to keep my voice stern. No sense in letting him sense my fear.

"I'm just ... checking up on some of the details of your excavation." Luke nodded firmly. "Frances's notes weren't very expansive. I thought I'd come here and try to get a sense of things *in situ*."

"This area of the cave hasn't been explored," I said, my voice shrinking in the cavernous space. "That fact was in the notes you were reading. It's dangerous to come here by yourself, especially at night, especially if no one knows where you are."

"You know where I am," he growled, those fierce green eyes flickering over my body. With a flush, I remembered that I was wearing my hideous pink thermal leggings underneath my Snoopy pyjama pants. Could this day get any worse?

"We shouldn't be in the caves at night," I repeated nervously. "I believe a certain ranger told me it's against the rules."

"Do you ever do anything that's against the rules?" he asked, closing the gap between us in a heartbeat. He still hadn't touched me, but my body flooded with warm, pulsing energy. How was it he could make me feel this way? Especially when I'd just caught him red handed doing something he shouldn't.

"I ... er ..."

"I thought so." Luke stepped closer. "Anna, I can explain. I—"

"Argh!" I screamed as something swooped down from the darkness and flapped beside my face. I dropped my torch as I flung my hands up to protect my eyes from the screeching bat. My stomach turned as the bat's furry body slipped through my fingers and scrambled into my hair, its wings twitching as it tangled itself deeper.

The torch clattered on the rocks below, bouncing down the steps and plunging into the pool. The light went out.

"Fuck," Luke swore. "Stand still!"

"I can't stand still. There's a bat in my hair!" I wailed, flailing my hands around my head. I turned to run back down the fissure, but instead I crashed into Luke, sending his torch flying from his hands. It hit the rocks with a crash, and the light flickered out, plunging us both into complete darkness.

Tears welled in my eyes. The bat's feet scrabbled against my head, yanking my hair so hard the entire side of my scalp felt as though it were being pulled off. Luke's hands battled in my hair. He swore again as the squabbling intensified. Finally, the bat released me, and I heard its wings flapping away into the darkness.

"Ow." I touched the side of my head. My scalp felt tender. But at least it was still there. Luckily, I'd already had a tetanus shot.

"Anna, are you okay?"

I nodded, biting my lip. After a moment of silence, I realised how stupid that was. "I'm fine," I said, my voice cracking.

"I can tell. Here, hold on to me," Luke ordered. I reached out, grabbing for his elbow, but instead, my fingers brushed the fabric of his jeans. I felt the button on his fly. Shit. I'd grabbed him right—

"If you wanted an excuse to grope me, you just had to ask," he said, laughing.

"Shut up," I shot back, heat flaring in my cheeks. I was lucky it was so dark, he wouldn't be able to see how beet-red I must be. I reached up, clamping my hand around his forearm. The warm sensation raced through my fingers, down my whole arm, lighting all my senses on fire.

Woah. The heat was intense. It wasn't just my hormones on overdrive. The heat penetrated every layer of my body, spreading through my limbs and circling through my head. My chest swelled with intense emotion. I gulped back the urge to ... I'm not sure whether I wanted to cry or laugh or kiss Luke or push him away or beg him to marry me. The intense sensation swirled around my head, and in the darkness, it was even more disorienting. I squeezed Luke's arm tighter, reassuring myself that he was there, and that I was standing upright still.

"Luke," I asked, tugging at my hand. "I feel—"

"I know." His deep voice came through the dark. Confident, reassuring. "Don't think about it right now, Anna. We need to focus on getting out of here. Can you follow behind me?"

"I ... I think so."

Luke's fingers closed around mine. The warmth in my body surged. Slowly, Luke felt his way back up the fissure, squeezing his way between the gap. I kept close at his heels, my other hand feeling my way along the rocks, re-establishing my bearings. Every few moments he squeezed my hand. I squeezed back, assuring him I was fine.

"You're good at this," I remarked as we emerged onto the site and Luke picked his way carefully around the quadrants without disturbing any of our cuttings.

"I can see well in the dark," he said, then sucked in his breath, as though he'd said something he shouldn't.

"That's interesting."

"Is it?" He slid down a rocky ledge, then turned to grip my waist with his strong hands. Before I could say anything, he'd lifted me down, and crushed my body against his powerful chest. My face was millimetres from his. His hot breath warmed my lips. The energy between us sizzled. "I can think of much more interesting things right now."

Kiss me, my body screamed. In the dark, my senses worked in overdrive, assailing me with Luke's intoxicating masculine scent, the sensation of his fingers gripping me, the press of his bulge against my thigh.

"Luke—" I murmured, not sure whether I was protesting or begging.

"Anna." His husky voice grated against my ears. His breath caressed my cheek. And then, he pressed his lips to mine.

Want more? Read Digging the Wolf *if you love archaeological mysteries, badass wolves, a broken heroine, and a hero so hot he'll have you howling for more. Now FREE from your favourite ebook store!*

OTHER BOOKS BY STEFFANIE HOLMES

This list is in recommended reading order, although each couple's story can be enjoyed as a standalone.

Crookshollow Gothic Romance series

Art of Cunning (Alex & Ryan) - READ NOW FOR FREE

Art of the Hunt (Alex & Ryan)

Art of Temptation (Alex & Ryan)

The Man in Black (Elinor & Eric)

Watcher (Belinda & Cole)

Reaper (Belinda & Cole)

Wolves of Crookshollow series

Digging the Wolf (Anna & Luke) - READ NOW FOR FREE

Writing the Wolf (Rosa & Caleb)

Inking the Wolf (Bianca & Robbie)

Wedding the Wolf (Willow & Irvine)

Fallen Sorcery Fae (shared world)

Hollow

Witches of the Woods

Witch Hunter

Coven

The Curse (coming in 2018)

NEW FROM THE WORLD OF CROOKSHOLLOW

Sink your teeth into the hot new werewolf paranormal romance series from *USA Today* bestselling author, Steffanie Holmes!

Now FREE from your favourite ebook store!

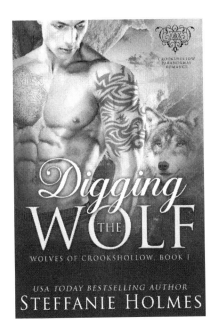

Anna

It's been five months since my boyfriend was tragically killed in a climbing accident. I didn't think I was over him ... until Luke walked on to the archaeological site.

Tall, dark, sexy, tattooed, funny, dangerous. Everything I want in a man.

But he's hiding something. He acts strangely in the moonlight. He won't tell me anything about his life. And I caught him trying to destroy an important find.

My body aches for him, but my heart tells me I'm not ready to make myself vulnerable again, especially not for a guy who isn't being straight with me.

If only ...

Luke

Anna Sinclair – archaeologist, geek girl, totally and utterly delectable.

I knew from the moment her intoxicating scent wafted across my wolf senses, she's meant to be mine.

And that knowledge is *terrifying*.

The last thing I expected was to find my fated mate on an archaeological site. Whenever I'm near her, all I want to do is claim her.

But she's broken. The last thing she needs in her life is a werewolf out for revenge. I'm here to destroy the site, to keep my family's past buried forever.

If Anna finds out the truth, she'd never speak to me again.

But I can't deny the bond between us. **I'll do anything to make her mine.**

Digging the Wolf is a standalone paranormal romance by USA Today bestselling author Steffanie Holmes. Read if you love archaeological mysteries, badass wolves, a broken heroine, and a hero so hot he'll have you howling for more.

Start reading on steffanieholmes.com

SUPPORT ME ON PATREON!

*Y*ou can support Steffanie's writing via her Patreon page – it's like an ongoing crowdfunding campaign where you get free books, deleted scenes, random fun stuff, and the chance to name characters and decide plots.

Check out Steffanie's patron page at: www.patreon.com/steffmetal.

ABOUT THE AUTHOR

Steffanie Holmes is the author of steamy historical and paranormal romance. Her books feature clever, witty heroines, wild
shifters, cunning witches and alpha males who *always* get what
they want.

Before becoming a writer, Steffanie worked as an archaeologist and museum curator. She loves to explore historical settings
and ancient conceptions of love and possession. From Dark Age
Europe to crumbling gothic estates, Steffanie is fascinated with
how love can blossom between the most unlikely characters.

Steffanie lives in New Zealand with her husband and a horde
of cantankerous cats. She also writes science fiction and urban
fantasy under S. C. Green

Steffanie Holmes Mailing List

*Want to be informed when the next Steffanie Holmes paranormal
romance story goes live? Sign up for the VIP Readers Club to get the
scoop, and score a free book to enjoy!*

Come hang with Steffanie
www.steffanieholmes.com
hello@steffanieholmes.com

Made in the USA
Middletown, DE
11 July 2023

34846490R00139